AN INTIMATE ENCOUNTER WITH A TEEN-AGER
AND HER SEARCH FOR MATURITY

Phoebe was sixteen—sweet sixteen—when she realized there would be no turning back to childhood games. For she had ventured into the adult world with its compl... ... ...

She was ...

Desperate... ...

guide her ...

she had t...

whom she ...

of adolesce... ...her father—always controlled and remote—remained aloof. And dear, funny Paul, father of the unwanted child, who was so much the young boy discovering his maleness. Just two months ago life was safe, sunny and promising and the hours spent with him were a sweet exploration of love. Now there was only a raw, aching reality and the agonizing search for a way out . . .

PHOEBE—THE UNCOMMON STORY OF A GIRL'S PREMATURE CONFRONTATION WITH ADULT-HOOD.

PHOEBE
BY PATRICIA DIZENZO
Adapted from the film PHOEBE produced by
the National Film Board of Canada

BANTAM PATHFINDER EDITIONS
TORONTO / NEW YORK / LONDON

A NATIONAL GENERAL COMPANY

PHOEBE
A Bantam Book

PRINTING HISTORY
McGraw-Hill edition published September 1970
Bantam Pathfinder edition published August 1970
2nd printing

Based on the film PHOEBE *produced by the*
National Film Board of Canada

All rights reserved.
Copyright © 1970 by Bantam Books, Inc.
This book may not be reproduced in whole or in part, by
mimeograph or any other means, without permission.
For information address: Bantam Books, Inc.

Published simultaneously in the United States and Canada

Bantam Books are published by Bantam Books, Inc., a National
General company. Its trade-mark, consisting of the words "Bantam
Books" and the portrayal of a bantam, is registered in the United
States Patent Office and in other countries. Marca Registrada.
Bantam Books, Inc., 666 Fifth Avenue, New York, N.Y. 10019.

PRINTED IN THE UNITED STATES OF AMERICA

PHOEBE

1

PHOEBE WAS sleeping late again. Her bedroom was light now even with the shades drawn. It was past ten. Her shorts and striped polo shirt lay on the floor, along with a pink beach bag and two dirty white sneakers she had kicked off before she fell into bed.

Something was wrong with the room. It wasn't just the clothes on the floor. On the dressing table, a neat row of bottles and jars had once lined up against the mirror. Now there was a chaos of perfume and powder and lipsticks. Some talcum powder had spilled over the table. A bottle of cologne was missing its cap. A raggetty-ann doll on the bookshelf, fallen on her side over a copy of *The Catcher in the Rye*, looked around unhappily, as though she could remember better days.

Phoebe had come in late the night before—past two. She and Paul had gone to the lake again, then to the old cabin they'd found. "Our house," as Paul called it. By the time they started for home it was dark; they'd had trouble hitching a ride on the highway. Her mother and father must have been in bed for hours when she let herself in the front door and tiptoed up to her room. Her father slept soundly, but her mother might have heard her. If so, she hadn't said anything. Well, she'd soon know.

She frowned in her sleep and shook her head, as if to say no. She didn't want to wake up. She rolled over, burying her face in her pillow. In a moment she was smiling faintly. She was having a dream—a dream she'd had before.

In the dream she walked into the living room where her mother and father were talking. They stopped when they saw her standing in the doorway, and looked up expectantly.

"Mother—Dad—" she began. "I have something very important to tell you—it isn't easy."

They waited. Her voice was trembling with nervousness. This was going to be so unexpected.

"I'm going to have a baby!" she said.

For an instant her mother's face showed disbelief. Then it lit up with joy. "Darling, how wonderful!" she said, and ran across the room and hugged her.

"This is news, my dear," said her father, putting down his pipe and giving her a kiss.

Her parents sat her down between them. Her father put a cushion behind her back, already concerned about her condition. His daughter deserved the best care he could give her, starting now! Mother, as usual when she was excited, began to make plans. "Now your room won't be big enough for you and the baby—we'll have to do something to fix up the den, don't you think, Arthur? Get the television out of there . . . Now, have you started to think about names, Phoebe? I used to have a book. I wonder if it's in the attic. Now if it's a boy . . ."

She stopped. Her husband and Phoebe were laughing. She laughed herself and gave her daughter another hug.

"You have to understand your old mother—I mean, the

new grandmother," she said. "I don't get news like this every day."

"Well, you certainly make us proud of you," said her father. "This means a lot more to us than your getting into college."

"You've always made us proud of you," said Mother. "We were just talking about that when you came in, weren't we, Arthur? But this is really special."

"You know, I was a little nervous about telling you," said Phoebe, smiling.

"Oh, darling. How silly of you. You know you can tell us anything, even if it were bad news."

Such a warm family!

"Phoebe! What's the matter with you?"

Her mother's voice broke into her sleep. Something was wrong. She didn't sound proud, or at all pleased with her. She sounded annoyed.

"Phoebe! Why don't you answer me? Are you still asleep? I said there's a phone call for you!"

Phoebe listened, half asleep, trying to figure out how Mother could possibly be annoyed with her.

"I don't know what to do about you any more. What time did you get in last night? You don't even get up in the morning. Do you think that's decent for a girl your age?"

"Is it the phone?" Phoebe mumbled.

"What?" her mother shouted. "Will you get up and answer the phone? It's your boy friend again."

Phoebe got out of bed and walked barefoot in to the hall, holding her head. It was splitting. Her mother was standing at the bottom of the stairs, watching her.

"What's wrong with you?" asked Mrs. Altman.

"Tell him I'll call back," said Phoebe. She saw her mother's tired face at the bottom of the stairs. She was holding a dish towel. She looked angry.

3

She was awake now, but she felt dizzy. She had felt this way before. Just like she'd had that dream before.

Suddenly she slapped her hand to her mouth and ran to the bathroom. There she fell to her knees, and vomited into the toilet. Then she sat still, waiting for it to happen again. It did. She closed her eyes, holding her head in her hands. She could feel beads of perspiration on her forehead. Her head was clearing and a feeling of coolness came over her face.

This had all happened before. Yesterday morning, the day before, and once last week.

"Phoebe," her mother called from downstairs. "If you want any breakfast, you'd better hurry up."

She couldn't answer right away.

"Do you hear me, Phoebe?"

"Yes," she said, almost in a whisper.

"Phoebe, what's the matter with you?" She could just see her mother standing at the foot of the stairs, deciding whether or not to come up.

She got up and walked out to the hall and stood at the head of the stairs. "Nothing's the matter with me," she said irritably. "Can't a person even cough in this house?" Her feeling of sickness had passed. She felt almost strong enough to go down to breakfast and face her mother.

She went back to the bathroom, flushed the toilet, then looked at herself in the mirror as if to find signs that she had changed.

She tried to look at her reflection as at a stranger. She was of medium height, and in her pajamas her figure looked a little boyish, though it had started to fill out over the last couple of years. She wasn't aware of it, but her movements had changed too during that time, become slower and more graceful. She was tanned from the long summer days at the lake; the light freckles on her nose didn't show any more. Her dark hair fell down to

4

her shoulders in two bunches, held by rubber bands. It had started to come loose in her sleep. She reached up to pull out the bands, still staring at herself.

She didn't look different. She looked like she did a month ago, or last fall when she and Paul had first started going together. She was only fifteen then. Now she was sixteen. She moved her fingers across her cheeks and under her eyes. They looked back at her, dark and quiet, telling her nothing.

Her mother called again, telling her to hurry and come to breakfast.

She was awake now. It was Sunday, thank goodness. She could see the day unfolding ahead of her.

She would meet Paul again, and they would go to the beach, and maybe to the cabin again. They would probably have to hitch a ride again. In a minute she would go down to the kitchen and see her mother, who was angry with her again. At night, if she stayed home, she might hear her parents argue about something. Or maybe things would be okay. Maybe Mother would tell Dad how late Phoebe came in last night. Maybe Dad would say something to her.

The day was beginning. She no longer smiled; the dream had faded away completely. She brushed her teeth and splashed cold water on her face. Only one part of the dream was true and wouldn't go away. She had known for several days now that she was going to have a baby.

2

"I wish you could get up—just once—in time to have breakfast with your father and me," said Mrs. Altman. "He never even sees you any more."

"He must really be suffering," muttered Phoebe, buttering a second piece of toast.

"What was that? Don't talk with your mouth full."

"I said," repeated Phoebe, raising her voice, "Dad must be in great suffering not to see me when he has his breakfast."

"He would like to see you once in a while. He isn't just the one who pays the bills for you, you know—or maybe that's all he is to you."

"That isn't all he is to me," she sighed.

"And why aren't you eating your egg?"

"Because it's too raw! It isn't even cooked! For crying out loud, will you stop picking on me?"

Her appetite had been weird the last two weeks. All of a sudden she couldn't stand eggs. Or anything fatty. She cut every little piece of fat off the bacon on her plate, afraid of upsetting her stomach again. She took a third piece of toast and ate it without butter.

"It's cooked exactly like it's always cooked," her mother

went on. "Exactly four minutes by a timer, but to you it's raw!"

"Maybe I'm not in the mood today. Did you ever think of that?"

"Oh, you're not in the mood." Her mother sighed. "What *are* you in the mood for today? How about cleaning up your room? I should think you'd be ashamed—or do you expect me to do that too?"

Phoebe said nothing.

"I suppose you're going swimming again?" her mother persisted.

"That's right."

"With Paul, I suppose."

"Right, Mom," she answered sarcastically.

"And how are you going to get there?"

"Joanne's boy friend has a car."

"Well, that's strange. Joanne called last night and asked me to tell you she's going with her family to visit relatives today."

"Thanks for telling me."

"Phoebe, your father and I have told you a dozen times not to hitchhike."

"What's the matter with it?"

"What's the matter with it? We care about what happens to you even if you don't. All you have to do is read the papers to find out what's the matter with it. Young girls have been murdered..."

"I'm sorry, Mom. I don't have as much time to read the *National Enquirer* as you do."

"All right. That's enough! I don't like your attitude one bit! And I don't like what you've been up to..."

And you don't know the half of it, thought Phoebe.

"... and if you think I'm not going to let your father know the hours you come in at night—you missed two

7

days of school last week, but you feel well enough to run around at night. What time did you get in last night?"

"About eleven-thirty," Phoebe lied, looking down at her plate. "I think it was about eleven-thirty. I didn't look at the time."

Her mother said nothing.

Phoebe laughed. "Why don't you put in a time clock, Mom? Then I could punch in and you and Dad wouldn't ever be in the dark."

Her mother ignored this. "You were *not* in your bed at eleven-thirty, and you weren't in your bed at twelve-thirty either—and I know it because I was lying awake worrying about you."

"So why ask me?" yelled Phoebe. "You tell *me* what time I came in. You seem to know everything!"

"You may have come in at four in the morning, for all I know," said her mother. "I know the way you sneak up the stairs. I finally fell asleep."

"Then you couldn't have been too worried, Mother."

Her mother started to say something, then bit her lip, and left the room. Phoebe finished her dry toast, chewing slowly, staring at the breakfast table. The time she came in at night had been causing arguments in the Altman family for a few years now. Her parents complained about it as they did about taxes—and didn't seem to think there was much they could do about it. Phoebe had had a few years to think about the complaints and arguments. They had started when she was thirteen and beginning to go out Friday and Saturday nights with "the girls." Then they had become worse when she started going out with boys. She was sure what her parents really meant by all this criticism, even if they wouldn't come out with it. She could set it down like the axioms in her geometry book:

(1) They don't want me to have any fun. That's wrong, for some reason.

(2) They don't want me to grow up.

(3) The only thing that would really satisfy them is if I had no friends and never went out.

3

WHILE SHE waited for Paul, she tried to remember some of the serious talks they had had—times he had shown how intelligent and kind and understanding he could be. Often when they were together he just kidded around, but he had another, more serious, side; it was one of the things she loved him for, and it was more important to her now than it had ever been.

She sat on the front steps outside the house so he and her mother wouldn't run into each other.

"Hello, señorita!"

He greeted her with a Mexican accent, and kept it up as they walked toward the highway, even though she just sighed and said nothing. He didn't look her in the eye once he saw what a rotten mood she was in. He just kept talking faster in his own version of south of the border. He didn't sound as if he had ever had a serious conversation in his life.

He was a nice-looking boy, with an open face and a quick smile. His hazel eyes were never still; they always seemed to be darting around, looking for something. His sandy hair was shorter now that school had started—a compromise with his parents—but he still had to push it out of his eyes from time to time as he talked. He was of medium height, and well-built, but in his cotton knit shirt and blue jeans he looked like a boy, not a man. He never seemed to be still. He was too full of high spirits, or nervous energy, or whatever it was.

They stood at the side of the highway, trying to thumb a ride. A few cars passed them by, disappearing in the direction of Greenwood Lake. While Phoebe sighed, Paul played the bullfighter for comic relief.

"*Ai! Toro! Olé!*" he shouted, making passes at the passing cars. He looked like a poor prospect for a husband and father. Phoebe wasn't the audience he could have hoped for. "*Toro! Olé!*" he shouted as another car passed them. She watched him, and the car that whizzed by, absently.

"I'm glad to see it's not easy to crack you up today," said Paul, throwing himself into his act with more energy. "It just makes me try harder! *Toro! Toro!*"

Another car passed them. The highway was empty now. Paul scanned the horizon, shading his eyes with his hand.

"Your *mamacita* really hates me," he said flatly, in a Mexican accent right out of the movies.

"What do you mean? What did she say?"

"There is a big freeze on the phone when the great *torero* calls."

"You mean this morning? Did you get into an argument?"

"No arguments, señorita. She just says a broad saying such as, 'My daughter comes in late at night and disgraces herself,' and waits for me to volunteer the details."

Phoebe sighed. "You don't, I hope."

He had put his big striped beach towel around his shoulders like a cape.

"No details, señorita. *Mamacita* will have to get it some

11

other way. Your secrets are safe with me. I will protect you."

Phoebe laughed, but with no warmth. I will protect you, she thought. She had never felt so unprotected.

"Paul, I wish you'd drop that stupid accent."

"Are you kidding? They're paying fortunes to guys like me to go on TV. Can't you see me in one of those commercials, impressing a housewife? Have you ever seen anyone as good as me in any commercial—handsome and funny at the same time?"

Phoebe gave no sign that she heard him. There was a chill between them.

"Mother doesn't hate you," she said finally. "It's me she doesn't care for too much."

"I respectfully disagree. I think she hates me much worse than you."

Another car came into sight.

"Paul, maybe if you'd stop looking like an idiot, someone would stop for us."

He didn't answer her, but folded his towel over his arm and stuck out his thumb. The car slowed down a few yards past them.

"Are you going by Greenwood Lake?"

"Yeah. Get in." Paul took Phoebe's hand, and they climbed into the back seat. The driver, a salesman, looked at them, taking in their tanned young faces, their bright colored clothes, Paul's striped towel.

"Isn't it a little late in the year for swimming?" he asked.

"The water's still warm," said Paul.

"You kids have got the life," the man replied. "I've got half a mind to forget the trip today and spend a day at the lake myself."

"Well, I wouldn't if I were you," snapped Phoebe.

Paul laughed nervously. "Don't mind my sidekick," he

12

said. "She's mad because school started again, plus she's practicing so she can be a nagging wife when she grows up."

The salesman laughed.

"To each his own," he said. "I see all types in my line of work. I thought most girls today wanted to be career girls or hippies."

Phoebe wondered how she would ever get a job. She had seen TV shows and movies about career girls in New York. They all seemed to be having a great time. They had dates, tried new jobs, bought new clothes, met exciting new people, and generally whirled around the city in search of adventure. None of them had babies.

Paul and the salesman were talking about something. Phoebe tuned out, staring out the window at the filling stations, diners, and car lots they passed along the highway. She was going to tell Paul today, and talk seriously about what to do. She couldn't face the idea of telling her mother—or, even worse, her father—but it wouldn't come as such a shock to Paul. At least it shouldn't. And maybe he could think of something. After all, it wasn't just *her* problem. He was a man, really, or almost a man. . .

"It was a freak-out!" said Paul. He was describing a rock show they had gone to during the summer. Two singers had destroyed their guitars during their act.

"I'm working too hard. I ought to sell guitars," said the man. "The follow-up prospect ought to be pretty good if this idea catches on."

Phoebe sighed. Well, Paul wasn't really a man yet, but he might have an idea of what to do. She had been too upset to think at all. All her time had been spent hoping and praying it wasn't true. Would he offer to marry her? Some part of her hoped desperately that he would. It would mean he wasn't abandoning her. And yet she didn't know if she really wanted to get married. What would it mean? Paul quitting school, getting some kind of job. Would they get an apartment somewhere in town, or go somewhere, maybe California? Would she really drop out of high school? She had never even thought of that before. All her friends were finishing high school. In fact, half the kids in her class were going to college. Would she and Paul start hating each other? Maybe he'd blame her for ruining all his plans. . .

Just a few months ago she'd felt the world opening up to her. She was so excited about everything—school, being a senior, growing up, having dates—and now, suddenly, that time was over. The future had suddenly closed in on her.

She hadn't seen the danger. Somehow she had fallen into a trap, while all the time she had thought she was moving toward something good, something with Paul that would open up a new life to her. Now, so soon afterward, everything was closing in.

She felt as if she would start crying if she just kept sitting there.

"Paul," she said. "Let's walk the rest of the way."

He looked at her, surprised. "It's another half mile!"

"I feel like walking."

He could see she meant it, and didn't know what she might say next. The salesman slowed down and let them off at the side of the highway.

Paul looked at her. "All right. What's the matter?"

"I just wanted to walk."

"Something's the matter with you and you might as well come out with it."

"There is something," she said.

"What?"

"I don't want to talk about it now."

"Is it something at home?"

"No. In a way. I don't know. It's like it always is, I guess."

"Well, is it me? Is there something you want to say to me?"

"No."

"Do you want to break up with me? I've been wondering. If you do, you might as well say it. We can go home right now. It's better than you acting miserable all day, like you hate me."

"I don't want to break up with you."

It was funny to think he had been worrying about that. He put his arm around her shoulder, and they started walking.

"Do you ever think about breaking up with me?" she asked.

"Are you crazy? Of course not. But you've got to stop acting like this. I don't give a damn about that guy, but he must have thought you were crazy."

They walked on. The September day was warm, but not too hot. The sun felt good to her.

"You know, you get such a faraway look sometimes," said Paul. "I can never tell what you're thinking."

"Brilliant thoughts, don't worry. The world just isn't ready for them yet."

"When I daydream like that it's about you. But you don't think about me so much, do you?"

"Yes, I think about you a lot."

"Let's make up." He tightened his hand on her shoulder. "No one will be down there now."

It didn't make any difference. She couldn't be in any more trouble than she was already. Maybe she should at least be glad about that.

"I swear to God, Paul," she laughed. "Can't you ever get enough?"

"Don't talk like that. It sounds awful."

"What do you mean?"

"It just sounds so—so coarse," he said. "You never used to talk like that."

"I do a lot of things I never used to do."

"That's right," he said. "Make me feel guilty. You know—I ruined your life. If you'd never met me, you'd be the happiest girl in the world."

"I'm not saying it's your fault," she said. "I wanted to as much as you."

Or almost as much, she thought.

"I mean," she continued, "I was always attracted to you, but—I guess I don't understand you. Like—you seem to think about sex all the time."

"Well, don't you?"

"No. I mean, I think about you a lot. I think about sex. I always wondered about it, but it just seems with you, it's like—I don't know—constantly on your mind."

"Maybe you don't love me as much as I love you." He was hurt.

"I do," she said. "I just feel mixed-up about everything. Everything—my whole life—seems like it changed so fast, before I knew what was happening."

4

PHOEBE NEVER talked with her parents about sex. It would embarrass them, she could tell. In fact, knowing how they felt, she would probably be just as embarrassed herself. When she was eleven, her mother had given her a little booklet with a drawing of a fragile rosebud on the cover. It was entitled *Now That You're a Woman*— and it was designed to prepare her for the onset of menstruation, which it did. She read the booklet with interest and passed it on to her best friend Joanne. "It's a great masterpiece by Kotex," she said. Joanne laughed, sighing with boredom to equal Phoebe's, and read it cover to cover.

She knew, in a general, uncomfortable way, that her mother and father did not want her to "go too far" with sex. No doubt that was at the back of their minds when they criticized her for staying out too late, and Mother talked about her "running around." Mother had never once said she was glad Phoebe had a boy friend. (It was Phoebe's greatest fear, and Joanne's too, when they were twelve and thirteen, that boys would never like them.)

She was positive—she didn't have to ask—that her parents would be shocked if they knew what she and

17

Paul had done. But maybe they would hate her just as much for even thinking about it. Or for kissing. Or for liking boys at all. Or for being curious about what sex was really like. Or maybe they disapproved of the feelings of happiness she felt. Sometimes she felt so glad that she was growing up and could love someone so much. Sometimes she felt so full of happiness and excitement about life that it almost made her cry with gratitude. She probably wasn't supposed to feel that.

The only specific words of advice she had ever received on the subject of sex, and just how far a girl should go, came from Miss Dalton, the physical education instructor who taught a hygiene course. Miss Dalton put up diagrams of the male and female organs, discussed menstruation (a little late, as all the girls in the class were fifteen), and also got down to basics in one class. She discussed the extreme ease with which a girl could get pregnant. (With the diagram on the board showing millions of sperm cells making their way to the egg, one could hardly doubt her.) She then talked about the extremely strong sex drive of the seventeen- to nineteen-year-old male, and the increasingly tempting environment he lives in—miniskirts, erotic movies that teenagers can see, the freedom of having a date in a car, and the effect of all three combined.

Miss Dalton had then said that attraction between the sexes during adolescence was natural, and kissing, to a certain extent, was all right, but that "any girl who allows a boy to touch her breasts is asking for trouble, as it is very arousing to her and to the boy." And, she added, it is the girl who has to "apply the brakes."

If Phoebe had been able to accept Miss Dalton as an adviser, she would at least have had one person's advice about where to draw the line. But Miss Dalton didn't seem like a reliable source of information to her. She seemed quite strict, and not really a very warm person—possibly downright mean. Phoebe felt that deep down she probably completely disapproved of sex, but just wouldn't come out and say so, as she knew it wouldn't go over very well with the girls. Miss Dalton had never married and wasn't Phoebe's idea of the woman she wanted to become.

She didn't know exactly what kind of woman that was. It wasn't her mother; her mother didn't seem very happy most of the time. Her life was "all right:" No better, no worse. Phoebe had some vague ideal—she didn't know where she got it—of a woman who was married, and in love with her husband, really in love with him, and had children but didn't feel burdened down by them, and who still laughed once in a while and was interested in the people she knew and different things in her life. And part of the picture, running underneath everything, was that the woman was sexual, that this was at the center of her life. From what Phoebe could tell, the center of Miss Dalton's life was gym class, and Phoebe hated gym.

For the last six months Phoebe had marked a calendar to keep track of her periods. She used just to keep the dates in her head, but since she started sleeping with Paul she knew it was important to know exactly when she was due. She kept the calendar, with its circled days, between the pages of a book on her bookshelf, an old Nancy Drew mystery called *The Secret in the Old Clock*. She didn't want her mother to come across it as she was sure it would be a dead giveaway. Her periods were fairly regular, usually coming every thirty days. She had never skipped one since she was thirteen. Then, at the end of July, two months ago, she was late. She tried not to worry. She had heard nerves could hold it up. She took hot baths. She had heard quinine water would bring it on. She bought two bottles and, sitting alone in her bed-room, drank them down in one night. Nothing happened. She told herself she was just panicky and it was upset-ting her whole system. She could hardly believe it when the fortieth day came and went. Along with a feeling that it couldn't be real, she felt a chilling sense of fear. She sat in a hot tub for hours, trying to read a book. Her breasts were a little tender and swollen, but they often were immediately before her period. She tried to take it as a good sign.

I'm just upset, she thought. It's obvious that's what it is. It's an awful vicious cycle. If I could just relax and stop worrying, it would come tomorrow.

She was frightened, but the probable truth was still too strange and terrifying to sink in. It was impossible. She was still in high school. She didn't want this to hap-pen to her. She still wore knee socks and loafers. She was too young to be a mother. Nature just wouldn't let it happen now.

When she was two weeks late, she suddenly had an idea: I've just skipped a month, that's all. It happened once a few years ago, before I started getting regular.

The thought comforted her. She took out her calendar and circled the day, already two weeks past now, when she should have started menstruating. It was August 9. Then she counted thirty days from that. She was sure her period would come then—September 10. She pinned her hopes on that. She didn't worry too much as another week passed. Soon it was fifty days since her last period. Then fifty-one, fifty-two...

School started September 8. It was her senior year. Somehow she had always thought it would be the best of her life. But her new schedule, the new books and courses, the new teachers, held no interest for her. She registered these things mentally but had no feelings about them one way or another. One thing alone interested her. She had cramps every day. She was overjoyed, feeling sure it was the sign everything was all right. But nothing happened. After a few days the cramps stopped, just as if she'd had her period and it was over for another month.

The second week of school she missed a day because she was sick in the morning. She had heard about morning sickness but told herself it was just another sign of the terrible tension building up in her.

I have such a crazy imagination, she thought. I've always been too emotional for my own good.

She missed a Tuesday, then half of the next day, going in on Wednesday afternoon with a note from her mother. She was afraid of being absent and people beginning to wonder what was wrong. The nausea usually came over her when she first got out of bed in the morning. She started setting the alarm for six-thirty, thinking she could get it over with and then be all right by eight-thirty, when she had to leave for school. She was always awake before the alarm went off. She never knew exactly when she woke up. It seemed as though she had been staring at the clock all night, her mind dull with worry.

Getting up early worked quite well. Her parents didn't hear her in the bathroom, and it helped her make it to school, except for a couple of days when the queasy feeling just wouldn't pass. She dreaded the idea of getting nauseous in class or in the halls.

She took a hot bath every night. She stared at the calendar, watching September 10, and the days after it, come and go. She was late now even if she *had* skipped a period.

All this time she was going to school (nearly every day), sitting in her classes, taking gym, talking to friends, doing her homework as best she could. She saw Paul and her parents every day, but she was very alone.

5

"PAUL, YOU'VE never told anyone about us?" she asked. They had changed into their bathing suits—or rather, peeled off their outer clothes—and were lying on the beach.

"Of course not."

"Because I don't want to become a school legend like Arlene Miller."

He looked at her, puzzled and annoyed.

"I won't," he said shortly. "You didn't have to ask."

"I'm sorry." She grabbed his hand and kissed it. "I'm just turning into a crab like all the women in my family. I can't let down the great family traditions."

"Forget it." Paul laughed. He lay on his back, his eyes closed under his sunglasses.

They lay quietly for a while. Phoebe stared at him. He was young. He wasn't solid; he wasn't sturdy and serious, with two feet on the ground, like her father. But he never meant to hurt her. He just never thought it would happen. He never thought. . .

The sun made her feel good, not so tense as she'd felt all morning. The water looked beautiful, choppy and blue. The lakeside was almost deserted. Some way off she could see two small children with someone—probably their mother—playing in the sand with pails and shovels. She wondered how old the mother was. She looked again at Paul.

"Hey, Paul, you've got a hair on your chest!" she shouted suddenly.

He groaned.

"Don't wake me up for things like that. How many times have I told you?"

"But don't you want to know?"

"I do know. It's been there for five days, so please don't disturb me."

"But it's a sign of maturity, Paul! Maybe it will affect your whole personality."

"The Mackleys are all mature from the cradle. We're just not hairy."

"But still—it makes you seem older, more mature. Maybe you'll grow another before Christmas."

"I *am* going to grow another for Christmas, but what is the big hang-up you have about me being mature?"

"I don't have any hang-up about it."

"You know I'm as mature as they come. I've told you so a thousand times. I've told you about my career plans."

"No! You have career plans? The only one I know is when you wanted to be a cowboy."

"That was long ago, when I was a junior, my dear, and wanted to smoke Marlboros. My plans now are not to smoke at all and to be an astronaut."

"Oh, an astronaut—that's terrific—a beautiful idea." She meant to keep on kidding, but there was a disappointment she couldn't keep out of her voice.

"You hate it. I can tell. I thought you'd be glad I finally decided."

"You know, the competition's pretty tough, Paul. How many astronauts are there anyway? About ten? And there

23

are two hundred million people in this country and about half of them want to be astronauts."

"I'm convinced I can beat them all out, Phoebe. Don't you have any confidence in me?"

"Yes. You'd probably make it." She turned away from him, looking at the water. One of the children had found a rock, and was throwing it into the water. "Then you go through twenty years of training and end up dead on the moon."

"Phoebe, this conversation about my career is getting me down. Let's talk about sex."

"Well, that might get *me* down."

"Why? Are you against it all of a sudden?"

"Paul, I swear to God, I think you're abnormal."

"Me? Abnormal? You don't know anything! You're completely ignorant about this. . ."

I'll say, she thought.

"Don't you know what's in the Kinsey Report?"

"How would I know? It's on the locked shelf at the library and for some strange reason my mother forgot to give me a copy my last birthday."

"Well, Pete Dranner's brother has a copy and this is a book that would open your eyes. The things that are going on all over this country—this very minute—well, they make me look like the world's biggest square."

"What do you mean?"

"Everyone is a sex maniac compared to me. They do things I never even thought of! And those country guys—you know how they look so innocent on television, playing the guitar, smiling? Listen, there are statistics on them. These guys are willing to try anything once."

She started to laugh, but stopped midway and slapped him on the arm.

"Oh, Paul—shut up! What do you think I am? One of the boys?"

24

He laughed, rolling away from her.

"Who's going to tell you if I don't?"

She missed as she tried to hit him again.

"I don't know. No one! I don't want to listen to that! Is that supposed to make me feel better about my life?"

"Don't be afraid of the truth!"

"I don't need the truth if that's what it is."

She sat back again and brushed the sand off the blanket.

"Let's go in the water, Phee. It's hot."

"No, I don't want to."

"Oh, come on. It's beautiful."

"No, I'm not kidding. I'm just going to lie here and take a nap."

"All right then, I'm going in. By the way, you're really a lot of fun today."

He jumped up and ran into the water. She lay there, looking at him swim and splash around. She almost wanted to join him, but felt too weary to make the effort. She rolled onto her stomach, resting her face in her arms. Paul was smart, she thought, and full of energy—and optimistic, and always had a lot of ideas. Maybe he could take the bad news better than she had.

She imagined him still lying beside her on the blanket.

"I'm sorry I've been such a pain in the neck this morning," she said. *"It's just because I'm worried about my pregnancy."*

Paul's face lit up—just as Mother's had in the dream she had last night.

"Pregnancy? Why didn't you tell me, Phoebe? You mean I'm a father? And you're going to be a mother?"

"Yes. I think it will be about Easter time."

"Oh, Phoebe, that's fantastic! Oh, I love you so much!" He put his arms around her and held her close.

"But—but aren't you worried about what your family

25

will say?" she mumbled. *"Aren't you worried about your college plans?"*

"Look. They'll just have to understand. And I'll have to get a job and go to night school. It'll be hard, but I'll have something to work for. . ."

"Oh, Paul, I was so afraid to tell you. I know it probably sounds silly, but I was afraid you'd be upset."

"Of course I'm not upset. I'm very happy about it, dear."

Dear! He sounded so much older when he called her that.

She smiled, then laughed at herself. Paul was floating on his back out past the ropes. She could see his red swimming trunks flash as the water lifted him up and down. She got up from the blanket and ran into the water, swimming out to him. He couldn't hear her call his name, and was surprised when she swam up to him and touched his arm. He looked as though he'd forgotten his parting words.

"So you changed your mind. Isn't it great?"

"Oh, yes. It's still almost like summer. I was a little worried about you drifting out."

"You want to swim over to the raft?"

"Okay."

They reached the raft, she slightly behind him. He climbed up on the wet boards and walked around, shaking the water off him. She stayed in the water, holding onto the side.

"I wish we had a ball or something," he said. "Hey, here's a Coke can."

"Well, don't throw it at me and knock me unconscious," she said. "I'd be another American tragedy—drowning in a lake after being struck by a can of Coke."

An American tragedy. Wasn't that a famous book, a movie she'd seen on television where a man drowned his girl friend in a lake because she was pregnant? She couldn't seem to control the drift of her thoughts.

"You're very morbid today, Phoebe. I'm going to have to duck you."

He took a running jump from the raft and jumped into the water with a giant splash. She swam back toward the shore.

"I take it back! I'm happy! I'm not going to drown! I'm never going to die!"

"All right. That's more like it. I'll let you off this time."

He had caught up to her and grabbed the bathing suit strap around her neck, but now he released it. She shook her head to get the wet hair out of her eyes, treading water.

"How about going in?" he said, grabbing her hand.

"All right."

"Let's go in the cabin. I've got a beyoo-tee-ful tune I want to play for you on our piano."

"Oh, I don't know. . ."

"Look, we have to change somewhere, don't we?"

"Sure," she said. "Okay."

They swam back and picked up their things at the blanket. It was only a short walk to the cabin.

It was an old place, really larger than a cabin because there was a second floor, sort of like a loft, under the slanting roof. Once it had seemed a warm and friendly place to Phoebe. Looking at it now, she saw only a cold, lonely house. Its gray shingles were streaked and weatherbeaten by the dampness and the wind from the lake. No light came from the shaded windows. Tall grass and weeds sprouted from the sandy soil around the front porch. There was something strange, almost sinister, in the feeling of stillness that surrounded the place.

A low wooden fence surrounded the bare yard. The gate was locked but it was easy to climb over, as they

27

had done before. Paul jumped over the low railing and ran around to the back. Phoebe stood by the gate. She moved her lips faintly as if to call him back, but then said nothing and climbed over herself.

The back door was still unlocked. Paul pushed it open and walked into the main room. His footsteps made the old floorboards creak, setting off tiny echoes in the almost empty rooms. Phoebe remembered how, when they first sneaked into the house, they were convinced someone else was there. She remembered how her heart quickened at the thought, and how it quickened again when she realized no one was there, that they were alone in the house.

The main room was empty except for an old piano and, surprisingly, a telephone still in working order. It was as if someone had left in a hurry, expecting to come back to finish the job, and never had.

"Yoo hoo!" yelled Paul, cupping his hands around his mouth. Echoes came back from the other room and from upstairs. They used to yell a lot in there, listening to the echoes bounce back from the empty corners. They had run around the first floor, and up and down the stairs, laughing breathlessly, finding hiding places and trying to take each other by surprise. She remembered feeling very playful and at the same time more and more serious. They had been coming closer and closer to sleeping with each other before that, and when they found the empty house they both knew it was a perfect place. It all seemed a long time ago.

A family once lived here, she thought. I wonder what happened to them?

"I'm going upstairs and getting out of this wet suit," she said.

"Aren't you getting a little coy all of a sudden? Can't I help?"

"No—really, I'll be right back. My teeth are chattering."

"Whatever you say." He sighed, turning away from her. As she ran up the stairs she heard him picking out a tune on the piano. Now that she was out of the sun, her bathing suit was cold and uncomfortable, and she was glad to get it off. She looked down at her stomach as she put on her underwear. There was no swelling at all. No one would ever think she was pregnant, even if they were on the lookout for it. When did it start to show? She thought it was about the fourth month; maybe not *too* much even then—unless someone were looking out for it. She started thinking in a very practical way about school. She could wear full skirts, some jumpers with high waists; that might get her through Christmas. . . .

As often happened these days, she felt a sudden rush of fear. So often she could keep it at bay. She could stay fairly calm, think practically about ways to hide her symptoms, even think about other things, and laugh with Paul—and then the fear would come back in a rush. It was as if she had turned a corner and suddenly, without warning, come face to face with something so terrifying that she couldn't even move or call for help.

Her hands were shaking so badly that she couldn't manage the buttons on her blouse. She kept trying, then gave up, sitting down on the iron cot and waiting for it to pass. It was really true. She was going to have a baby and she couldn't stop it. It was her body but she had no control over what was happening inside her. She pressed her hand on her stomach, wondering if she could feel anything inside. There was nothing. It was a secret she was keeping from everyone, but in a few months it would be impossible to hide—no matter what she said, no matter what she did, no matter what kinds of clothes she wore.

She heard the piano downstairs. Paul was picking out

a tune she couldn't recognize. He was probably mad at her.

She imagined him sitting at the edge of the cot, where he'd sat at her side so many times before.

"Paul," she whispered, looking across the room at the other empty cot. "I'm going to have a baby."

The Paul in her mind's eye looked down at the floor and said nothing.

"What are we going to do?" she asked, trying to hold back her tears.

"What am I supposed to say?" he asked. "Hurray? And I'll tell my parents? And they'll kick me out of the house, but that's okay? I won't finish high school, I won't go to college, but that's terrific? I'll get some lousy job that pays forty dollars a week and we'll live happily ever after?"

"I'm sorry." She broke down and started sobbing.

"You can't blame me for it," he said. "It was you as much as me. I never forced you."

"But it was both of us," she said, trying to keep her voice steady. "It was both of us—it's not fair for me to bear it all alone. . ."

"And it's okay that my life is ruined?" he shouted. "Maybe you did this to trap me! Maybe you're sick of school. Maybe all you want is a husband and a baby."

"But I don't want a baby," she protested.

"And I don't want to get married!"

Her mouth was dry as she whispered to the empty room, "I didn't want to get married anyway."

She picked up the wet bathing suit from the floor and wrapped it in her towel. She buttoned her blouse slowly, then shook the sand out of her sneakers. She could still hear the piano downstairs. She looked at the empty cot across the room as though her daydream had really just taken place there. Surely Paul wouldn't talk to her like that.

She combed her hair, using an old speckled mirror hanging on the back of the door. She looked curiously at her reflection, as she'd been doing lately. She couldn't tell if she looked different or not. She put on her sneakers, picked up her things and went downstairs. Paul came over to her, put his hand on her shoulder, and kissed her on the cheek.

"I'm sorry if I said anything to get you mad, Phoebe."

"Oh—it's all right. I'm just jumpy."

"Wouldn't you like to go upstairs? Please. It's still early."

"Paul—I—I—can't. I mean, I don't feel well. I didn't want to say anything but—well," she blurted out. "I have cramps. My period is late."

It was so easy! She had told him, or practically told him.

"Oh, that's too bad," he said. He seemed disappointed but not worried.

"It's nothing serious," she said.

"Oh, I know. I'm just sorry."

She waited for him to say something more. He didn't seem to know what she was telling him. Was he so far from the reality of what she had to live with day in and day out that the words "my period is late" didn't even ring a bell with him? Surely he knew what it could mean. But he obviously hadn't thought of it. She was half relieved, half confused.

"Then do you want to go home or in the water again?" he asked.

"I guess home," she said. "I've got homework and I don't want to stay up all night with it."

"Okay. You're the boss."

"Oh, listen. I forgot about the food." She opened up

her beach bag and took out some sandwiches. "I laugh while I make them, but if you like them—they're peanut butter and bacon."

"You're a doll," he said, biting into one. "I was starved."

They had a picnic on the floor. She was glad she had remembered to bring lunch because, strange as it seemed, she felt guilty about saying no to him. She had done it before and she had always felt guilty about it, as though she were letting down someone who needed her. The awful thing was that she felt just as guilty when she said yes. And now, when she thought about her parents discovering the trouble she was in, the guilt was too much to bear. She knew the shock it would be to them. It would come as an irreconcilable blow that their daughter, living with them under their own roof, had been leading a double life, one they had not even begun to suspect. But her feelings for Paul were strong too. No matter what she did, she never felt she was doing the right thing.

They walked home a good part of the way. Paul was in better spirits and started joking again about his career.

"Well, I just want you to understand one thing," she said, half seriously. "If you carry through with this, I won't necessarily be willing to marry an astronaut."

"Oh, it would be exciting and you know it," he said. "You'd be on television."

"I don't want to be on television and I don't want a husband who takes long trips."

"All right—if you don't want to stand by my side in my great life work, it's up to you. I never counted on your marrying me."

She laughed, then fell silent. It was true. He had never discussed marriage with her.

"Of course, you should have a great interest in the moon," he said.

"I do. How did you know?"

32

"I just figured, with all your loyal subjects there. . ."

He meant her name; Phoebe was the Greek goddess of the moon. She was the only girl in the school with that name. Her mother's younger brother had suggested it, she was told. He had showed up one night shortly before she was born, and disappeared soon after, sort of like a fairy godmother. He was supposed to be living in Italy now. "Crazy Harry," as her father usually referred to him. She had never seen him.

"How does it feel to be named after the goddess of the moon?" Paul asked, just to say something.

"It feels terrific," she said.

She felt very sad. Why did her father agree to the name if he thought her uncle was so crazy? After all, she was the one who had to live with it. Had there always been something different about her? She had always felt cut off. There was never anyone she could tell *everything* to. But she had taken that for granted, in a way. It never seemed so much a matter of life and death, as it did now.

She had thought all that had changed with Paul. Now she wondered how she could ever have believed they loved each other, understood each other, so much.

She admitted it to herself, dully; she was afraid to talk to him.

6

THEY WERE both getting tired walking, so Paul put out his thumb and they caught a ride home. The driver, a man about her father's age, talked with Paul about this and that. She said nothing the entire trip. When they reached the spot closest to her house, the driver slowed down and let them out on the side of the highway.

"Well, so long," she said to Paul.

"What's the hurry? I'll walk you home."

"No. I feel like walking by myself."

"I get it. And I suppose you don't want me coming over tonight?"

"No, I've got homework, I told you. I didn't do anything this weekend."

"I could bring mine over. No—forget it," he said, and walked away.

She started to call him, but decided to let him go. She didn't feel too good. She stepped over a low wire fence, went through someone's back yard, and so onto the sidewalk. She was only a few blocks from her house.

She walked slowly, looking at the houses with their mowed green lawns. The trees along the street were beginning to turn autumn colors. Fall had always been nice;

when she was a little girl it always meant the smell of burning leaves, and Daddy in the back yard, and new shoes for school. She kicked a few leaves, the first to fall, on the sidewalk.

Some children were playing stickball in the street. Others, too young to play, watched from the sidelines. One sat on her tricycle, ringing the bell on the handle bars from time to time, and staring intently at the players. Another girl, probably her older sister, sat behind an orange crate that was covered with a white cloth. Upon it rested two pitchers of identically red Kool-Aid. Business was slow, and her face brightened as she saw Phoebe approach.

"Do you want to buy some soda?"

Phoebe looked up from the sidewalk.

"What kind?"

"Cherry and strawberry."

"Which is which?"

The little girl paused for a minute. "What kind do you like?"

"Well, actually, I only like raspberry."

"That's this one," said the little girl, pouring from the pitcher on her left. "It's just like raspberry to a person who likes that kind."

This girl will never let herself get into my situation, thought Phoebe. She took the glass and started to drink.

"Do you have a lot of money?" asked the child, watching her.

"No," she said, putting down the glass. "How old are you, kid?"

"Eight. How old are you?"

"How old do you think?"

"About thirty-nine."

"Guess again."

"About thirteen."

35

"Wrong."

"Are you a teenager?"

Phoebe laughed. "Yes."

"I'm going to be a teenager!" said the little girl with a dazzling smile despite her missing teeth. Her younger sister nodded her head from her position on the tricycle.

"Well, lots of luck with it." Phoebe fished out a nickel from her pocket and paid the child. Turning to look at the children playing ball in the street, it seemed as though she would never again be as carefree as they were. And some of them weren't even that much younger. The oldest might be twelve or thirteen. Only three years or so since she had been the same age.

She rounded the corner. It was time to talk to her parents. They had to know sooner or later, and it might as well be now. But finding herself on her block sooner than she expected, she decided to walk around a little longer before going in. The morning's fight with her mother came back to her. This heart-to-heart talk was going to be unpleasant, to put it mildly.

She really hates me anyway, she thought; particularly the last couple of years. She's always criticizing me.

Yet the thought of telling her mother wasn't as bad as the idea of her father knowing. She could hardly bear to think of it. He was the one she had always wanted to please. He was the one she ran to when she had good report cards. Harsh words never flew between them, as they did between her and her mother. She loved her father, and she knew he loved her, but at the same time she was sure he didn't really *know* her. He thought of her as a little girl. He was going to be so shocked, so disappointed.

She didn't want to go inside, and stood a minute looking at the house. It was a pleasant-looking house, white with green shutters, shaded by two maple trees in the

36

front yard. The ground-floor window boxes were bright with flowers, yet it all looked as cold and forbidding to her as the cabin by the lake. It was her home but she was afraid to go inside.

The only thing that finally forced her to the front door was that there was no place else to go. Besides, she told herself as she reached it and the fear set in again, there's nothing to be afraid of. Never mind what you decided on the way home. You don't have to tell them now.

As she let herself in, she heard the ball game on the television in the den, a sign that her father was there. Making directly for the stairs, she walked as quietly as she could without tiptoeing. But in the upstairs hall, before she could get to her room, she ran into her mother.

"Oh, I'm glad you came home early, Phoebe," she said. Mrs. Altman had done her hair and had on her light green summer dress. She had just taken a shower and Phoebe could smell the dusting powder she had given her for her birthday. What was it? Friendship's Garden.

"We're going to go over to Betty's and Frank's for dinner. We're leaving in about a half hour. You'll have time to get dressed."

Phoebe just stared at her.

"Oh, you're going out to dinner?" she said dumbly.

"Well, we all are, honey." Her mother smiled. She seemed altogether different from the morning.

"I don't think I want to go, Mom."

Her mother had started to go into her bedroom. Now she stopped and looked at Phoebe. She was puzzled by something in her face, something in her voice.

"What's the matter, Phoebe? Have I been picking on you too much?"

"No."

"Are you still upset about this morning? I'm willing to bury the hatchet—how about you?"

"Oh, sure, Mom," she said. She had always enjoyed seeing her mother in a good mood. It made her seem so much younger, so happy. She sometimes forgot her mother wasn't even forty; she had been only twenty-two when Phoebe was born. When she wasn't tired from housework, or arguing with her father, or worried about money—or whatever she worried about—she seemed almost like an older sister.

"Come on—you'll have a good time. You always like to see Betty's children."

"I can't, Mom. I—I have homework."

"Is something wrong, Phoebe? Is it something at school?"

"No."

"Did you have a fight with Paul?"

"No."

"What is it then? You can tell me." She reached out to brush Phoebe's hair from her eyes, as she had done so often when her daughter was small. Unexpectedly, Phoebe began to cry, putting her head on her mother's shoulder.

"Oh, Mother, why am I such a brat?"

Mrs. Altman patted her shoulder a little uneasily. "You're not a brat. We've just been on edge this week. Somebody got up on the wrong side of the bed."

Phoebe said nothing, but didn't move away from her mother. It seemed funny to her that they were the same height now.

"You smell nice, Mommy," she finally said, trying to laugh but choking and breaking into fresh tears.

Her mother looked as though she didn't know what to make of it.

"Did you call me Mommy?" she asked, not knowing whether to laugh or not. "I don't think you've called me

38

that in five years. Listen, dear, we've got to leave soon. Why don't you put on your blue dress?"

"No—I—I really do have homework. I let it pile up over the weekend. I'll just make some spaghetti or a sandwich or something."

"Well, you could ask Joanne over, I guess."

"Yeah, maybe I will."

Her mother went downstairs. "Arthur," she heard her call. "We'd better leave. Phoebe doesn't want to go."

Phoebe went into her room, fell on her bed, and cried some more. It was hard enough to think of telling her mother when she remembered the fights they had had over the years, and the moments of pure hatred she had felt for her. But it was even harder when she thought of how much she loved her. Why couldn't she just be rotten all the time? Then it wouldn't be so confusing. It was the same thing with Paul. Her life had become a nightmare because of him, but she couldn't even hate him. Why couldn't people be all good or all bad? Paul was rotten, but he was nice too. If only he—and her parents—could be all bad, she could harden herself and keep her guard up. As it was, she never knew where she stood.

When her parents left, she ran a hot bath and soaked for almost two hours, trying to read her English assignment. She had to read the second act of *Romeo and Juliet*, which wasn't easy as she couldn't remember the first act. The past week had been so confused. She started at the beginning of the play, and tried to concentrate. The phone rang but she didn't get out of the tub. It was probably Paul and it was no use talking to him.

After two hours of keeping the water at the highest temperature she could stand, she got out of the tub and dried herself. Her skin was bright pink from the heat, and the water formed by the cooled steam was streaming down the bathroom mirror and tiles. These weren't just ordinary hot baths.

The ceiling will probably collapse from the moisture next week and kill me while I steam myself in here, she thought. Then my worries will be over.

She wrapped a towel around her and went to her parents' room, feeling the coolness of the world outside her steam room. It was a funny feeling to be walking around the house naked. She had always been modest with her father around the house, but lately she had felt the same way with both of them. She felt her body was a secret she had to keep to herself. She never even sat around in her room half dressed for fear her mother would come in without warning.

She took her mother's Friendship's Garden from her dresser and sprinkled it all over herself before she went to her own room and put on her pajamas and slippers. Then, as if to make peace with her mother in some more visible way, she put her room in order, picking up her clothes and tidying the bookshelf and dressing table. That done, she went down to the kitchen and made a sandwich, which she ate methodically, elbows on the table, with potato chips and a Coke.

By now it was close to eight o'clock. She went upstairs, lay on her bed, and again tried to read *Romeo and Juliet*. No use. She couldn't concentrate. It was all too sad anyway; she knew how it ended. She opened her history book and started to read the chapter Miss Andre had assigned Friday. It seemed crazy to be doing homework at a time like this, but she felt she had to keep her grip on school, on her normal routine. She was terrified of things beginning to slide away from her, getting out of control more than they had already. The pages blurred. It was something about the American Revolution, something about Boston.

She kept staring at the page with no sense of what it said. It might as well have been written in a foreign language. She went back to the beginning and tried again:

In 1773, Parliament passed the Tea Act, a law which . . .

She gave up and closed the book. It was only eight-thirty. She walked out into the hall and stood at the top of the staircase. She counted. There were sixteen steps going down to the front hall. She had once seen an old movie on television where a woman (was it Bette Davis?) who hated children, and hated her husband, found herself pregnant. She stood at the top of the staircase in her palatial new house and deliberately fell down the stairs. It brought on a miscarriage. Everyone felt sorry for her, not knowing she had done it on purpose. There was another movie too—a woman fell out of a car and lost her baby. It was awful to have to depend on Hollywood for information when you really needed to know. Was it true that women could lose their babies so easily? That a little fall would do it? But then did you bleed to death unless a doctor came? And did everyone know you had a miscarriage? She gripped the railing until her fingers ached. Her hand was cold and damp. She went back to her room and got into bed.

That night she dreamed that Paul had made a lot of money by appearing on a commercial for a new kind of floor wax, and had bought a house for them, with a nursery, somewhere in the country.

7

Normally, a woman realizes that she is pregnant because of the cessation of menstruation (amenorrhea). In the following weeks, this is confirmed by the swelling of the abdomen.

PHOEBE WAS sitting in a corner of the school library, reading Volume P of the encyclopedia. The heavy book, which she held slanted toward her, ready to snap shut at any moment, was open to the article on pregnancy. Every minute or so she looked up, afraid that someone might pass by and see the page. No one else was at her table. The library was fairly empty. Bruce Barker was sitting at the table next to hers, scribbling away at something, probably his history homework. She continued with her own research:

It is possible for menstruation to cease and for the abdomen to swell when there is no pregnancy. For this reason the physician must often use other criteria for his diagnosis . . .

She read the sentence again. Although she had guessed the truth about her condition two weeks ago, she was

42

still ready to believe she was wrong. Now the article said that all the sure signs came later—about the fourth month. That's when the doctor can hear the baby's heartbeat for the first time, or see his skeleton on an X-ray, or when the mother may feel the baby kicking inside her.

The fourth month. That would be about Thanksgiving.

She looked over again at Bruce, who showed no interest in what she was reading. She turned back to the page. She had never read the encyclopedia with such interest. Usually it seemed too dry, too full of unimportant little facts, but now every detail had meaning for her:

> Amenorrhea may occur in a woman who is not pregnant. Common causes are anemia and chronic infections such as tuberculosis. Another cause is emotional shock, such as the emotional shock that follows the death of a loved one, or the anxiety a woman may experience after exposing herself to the risk of an unwanted pregnancy.

Like me! Worried sick!

She reread this last sentence slowly. Then according to the encyclopedia, it could still be just a false alarm. And she didn't even have one of the worst symptoms; her "abdomen," as they called it, was not swollen.

She checked Bruce again out of the corner of her eye, and continued reading. That was all for the reassuring paragraph. The next went on:

> Feelings of nausea, which may or may not be accompanied by vomiting, are often experienced most strongly in the morning; thus the name 'morning sickness.' Morning sickness is a common symptom of pregnancy, occurring most often between the sixth and twelfth weeks.

Someone behind the bookshelf on her right pushed back his chair. She jumped nervously and closed the

43

book. She got out her history notebook and pretended to be poring over it, still checking Bruce—and over his shoulder, Pete Dranner, who was also busy with his history, scribbling notes as he read.

And why shouldn't he? What did Pete have to worry about? She remembered something Paul had said out at the lake, and imagined Pete poring over a ragged copy of the Kinsey Report. He looked just as interested now in history.

She sighed, and tried to concentrate on her history too. It was no use. She opened the encyclopedia again and stared at a diagram in the "pregnancy" article. The picture was captioned "Uterine Levels During Pregnancy." It showed the size and shape of a woman's womb at each month of pregnancy.

Phoebe looked at the line drawing, imagining it dressed in her high-waisted plaid jumper. The drawing confirmed what she had thought. The first and second months showed nothing. At three months it would still be fairly easy to hide. At four, it would be a problem, even with the right clothes. She certainly couldn't undress for gym in front of anyone. Anyone who was even a little suspicious—and by then a few people might be wondering why she was acting so strange and upset—would be able to tell, no matter what she wore. And at five months, a person would have to be blind not to notice.

The bell rang. She put the encyclopedia back on the shelf, picked up her books, and slipped the strap of her shoulder bag over her arm. Just one more class and the day would be over. She could go home and lie down.

History class was the same as always—discussion of the reading assignment with questions at the end. Miss Andre sat at her desk, looking down at her notes from time to time, then looking around the classroom with her sharp eyes.

Or were they sharp eyes? Maybe it's all my imagination, she thought.

Phoebe's history text lay open on her desk. She rested her chin on one hand, staring ahead at the dusty blackboard behind Miss Andre's desk.

Suddenly she imagined all the seats around her empty. She was the only one sitting in that room with the dusty blackboard, except for Miss Andre, who looked down at her papers, busily taking notes.

Phoebe approached the desk, and nervously cleared her throat. Miss Andre looked up.

"Yes?"

"Miss Andre..."

"What is it, Phoebe?"

"I'd like to talk to you about my work. I'm afraid I'll have to stop doing this history for a while."

"What do you mean?"

"Well, you see, Miss Andre, I just can't concentrate on it any more."

"Can't concentrate? Why?"

"Well—it's just that history seems so unimportant to me now. I have lots of other things to think about and plan for—and worry about. You see, I'm going to have a baby."

"Phoebe, you can't be serious."

"I was quite surprised myself, Miss Andre. I hadn't really planned on it."

"Well, I can certainly see why history doesn't interest you too much right now, my dear," said Miss Andre, patting Phoebe's hand. "I suppose we'll have to work out a special study plan for you."

"Oh, that would be very helpful..."

"When do you expect the child, dear?"

"Well—I don't know for sure. I'm really quite stupid— quite confused—about all this business of counting days— but I think I'm two months pregnant now, so that would

45

mean having the baby born in late April or maybe early May."

"Well, I'm glad to hear that, Phoebe. I'm sure you'll be up and around by June 17. You won't have to miss your graduation. That would have been such a shame."

"Yes—I hadn't thought of that."

"I think you'd better make plans to take a leave of absence from school sometime in January. It won't do to have you walking through these crowded halls between classes. And perhaps you'd better stop taking your gym classes very soon—perhaps after Halloween. If you like, I'll be glad to speak to Miss Dalton about that."

"It would be very nice of you, Miss Andre," said Phoebe. "Sometimes I don't know quite how to explain. . ."

"Of course. I'll speak to her. Now did you say you're two months pregnant?"

"Well, that's the funny thing, Miss Andre. I'm not positive. I've missed two periods. But I was just reading about it in the encyclopedia—right before history, as a matter of fact. I just couldn't keep my mind on the history reading, you see—I've suddenly gotten so interested in the subject of pregnancy. . ."

"Quite understandable," said Miss Andre. "But, my dear, may I give you one word of advice? The encyclopedia is a fine reference source, but you must feel free to talk to your parents and your doctor about any questions you have now. After all, a young girl shouldn't have to depend on an encyclopedia for a personal matter like this."

"Yes, I'm glad you reminded me of that, Miss Andre."

"By the way, Phoebe, who is the proud father?"

"Paul Mackley," said Phoebe.

"Oh, Paul," said Miss Andre. "I have Paul in my third

46

period class. A fine young man. I'm sure he's very pleased."

"I think so."

"Now. Let's meet down in the principal's office tomorrow and work out a home study course for you to cover those difficult months from January through April."

"Yes. I'll really work at home, Miss Andre. I don't want to fall behind. . ."

"What event led up to the Boston Tea Party? Phoebe?"

Phoebe jumped in her seat. Miss Andre was waiting for an answer. She felt as though she'd been asleep, but the words "What events led up to the Boston Tea Party?" still hung in the air.

"Oh—taxes," she said, hoping her voice didn't sound strange. "Taxes on tea."

"And what was the name of the law passed by the British Parliament in 1773 establishing this tax?"

Miss Andre waited. Phoebe said nothing.

"The Tea Act," said Miss Andre. "Now the Tea Act of 1773 was designed to aid what British trading company in its competition with the Dutch?"

How can I answer a stupid question like that? thought Phoebe. Don't you understand? For heaven's sake, I'm pregnant!

She answered meekly, "I—uh—don't know—the name of the company."

"The East India Company," said Miss Andre shortly. "Did you read the assignment?"

"Uh—yes—I did, Miss Andre."

She hoped no one would turn around and see she was more upset than she ought to be.

Miss Andre looked at her, said nothing, and made a mark in her book. Then, mercifully, she passed on to Pete Dranner, asking him something about the Sons of

Liberty. Phoebe didn't follow what he was saying, but she was sure he was making out better than she had.

She sighed, relaxing into her chair. She was safe for the rest of the period, as Miss Andre never struck twice in the same place. Pete's voice seemed to be coming from another planet.

Her mind was free again. There was no need to meet anyone's eyes. Again she imagined the classroom empty, except for herself and Miss Andre. Her history teacher was seated at her desk, making marks in her book. Phoebe got up from her desk and approached the front of the classroom. At the sound of her footsteps Miss Andre stopped working and looked up severely at Phoebe.

"Well, what do you want, Phoebe?"

"I—I'd like to talk to you about my work in history—and some other things, Miss Andre."

"Your work in history has been nothing short of a disgrace," said Miss Andre. "You should be ashamed of wasting the class's time, if not your own."

"I'm—I'm sorry about that, Miss Andre. I just haven't been able to concentrate. . ."

"You haven't been able to concentrate on American history?"

"Well, no—you know, usually it's very interesting, but now, well, right now, I have other problems. I haven't been feeling too well."

"I think I've heard that song before," said Miss Andre with a mirthless laugh. She tapped her pencil on her desk impatiently. "And just why haven't you been feeling so well?"

"I've been sick. . ."

"You look perfectly healthy to me."

"I—well, it's so hard to say, especially here in school,

but—I'm pregnant, Miss Andre. I've been worried sick ever since school started."

"I see." Her teacher's face expressed no emotion. Her voice was cold. "You've become pregnant and now you come to me asking for special treatment."

"Not special treatment. I was just trying to explain why my work hasn't been so good. . ."

"So good! Do you realize you're failing? Do you think you're going to graduate just because you show up and sit at your desk all day?"

With that, Miss Andre tore open her book and thrust it under Phoebe's nose. With a thin finger she pointed to the line opposite Phoebe's name. It was covered with a long line of tiny red zeros. Phoebe hadn't realized it was this bad. She couldn't keep from crying out.

"No!"

"And do you think you're going to be allowed to remain here—in your condition—in the same class with decent girls, fine decent girls who truly care about their educations. . ."

"Stop that, Miss Andre! You have no right to talk to me like that!"

"Oh, don't I?" Miss Andre put the book back on her desk.

"No—I just made a mistake."

"And do you think a decent girl, still in high school, would ever find herself in your situation?"

"It was just bad luck! Just a mistake. . ."

"Who knows how long you've had 'good luck' as you call it? But apparently things have finally caught up with you. We had a name for girls like you in my day. . ."

"You don't have any right to say that to me! I need help. You're my teacher, and you have to help me."

"My duty is to the students of this school, and you, my dear, have forfeited any right you ever had to remain a

49

student here. I shall, of course, have to go down to Mr. Duvane's office and inform him of this. I'm sure he will recognize his immediate duty to the students. You may be sure that you are going to be expelled."

"No!"

Phoebe smashed her fist on her teacher's desk. "Why is everyone else so perfect and right all of a sudden? Like I'm the only person in the world who ever made a mistake? Everyone's moving away from me as if I'm a leper—" Phoebe was angry and near tears. "I just made a mistake. A bad mistake."

Miss Andre carefully straightened the marking book on her desk.

"Don't raise your voice to me, young lady. If you had more self-respect none of this would have happened."

Phoebe imagined herself sobbing, throwing a ruler at Miss Andre, and running out of the classroom and out of the school.

The bell rang.

She shook her head, smiled faintly at her daydream, picked up her books, and headed for her homeroom. Eighth period was over and she had gotten through another day of school.

8

WHEN SHE got home the house was empty. At first she was just as glad not to see her mother—or rather, for her mother not to see her—as she was upset and probably showed it. But she was puzzled when she called to her from the hall and got no answer. She ran upstairs, then to the back door to see if she might be working in the yard. She wasn't there. Phoebe felt a growing uneasiness. It didn't cross her mind that her mother could be anywhere—out shopping, visiting a neighbor, at the dentist, any number of places. She was usually home after school, but it wasn't so unusual for her to be out. It was ridiculous to worry.

Yet here she was feeling like a small child who *must* know where his mother is, and is frightened when she is out of sight even for a minute. For years Phoebe had complained that her parents treated her like a child; all she had wanted was to be grown up. It was funny that now, when she was ready to become a parent herself, she felt more babyish than she had felt in years. It was the worry that did it. Having to go through this alone made her long for the days when life had been simpler, when she depended on her mother for all her needs, and trusted her, and had no secrets from her. Why had growing up made things so much more complicated?

She found the note on the dining-room table. She had put her books right beside it when she first came in and not seen it. It was in her mother's handwriting:

Phoebe:

Stevie had an accident this morning. I'm driving Betty and him to the doctor, as she is upset. I don't think it's too serious. Tell Daddy, and please make him some dinner. There's meat loaf from last night in the refrigerator.

Mother

She went up to her room and lay down on her bed. Betty was her mother's younger sister, and things like this had come up before. Her father wouldn't be too pleased to hear about it, she thought.

So she would be having dinner alone with him. She didn't know whether to be glad or not, but found herself hoping her mother would come home before he did. But five-thirty came, and she still wasn't there. Phoebe got up, washed her face and combed her hair, and went down to the kitchen.

Maybe this was lucky. It was a chance to talk to her father. She rarely saw him alone. Usually her mother was there, or else he was watching a ball game on television and didn't want chatter.

She put the meat loaf in the oven and started making a salad. She had given very little thought to the practical choices she was going to have to face. She thought and worried about how the people close to her would take the news—would they be furious, or would they be understanding? That, however, was only a small part of what was ahead of her. Whether they hated her or forgave her, they would still have to decide what was to be done. There were three possibilities she could think of, and she didn't know much about any of them.

The first was for Paul and her to get married, and support themselves and the baby somehow. That would mean not finishing high school. And she didn't know if Paul would want to, or if it would be the best thing. And maybe he needed his parents' permission at his age; she didn't know.

The second was to give up the baby for adoption. She knew that adoption agencies were supposed to screen couples to find ones who would make good parents. Then she'd never see the baby, and it would really belong to other people. But if she did that, where would she go? Just stay at home, hiding from the neighbors until it was time to go to the hospital? Would her father possibly know about these things? Maybe he'd be willing to find out.

And there was abortion. She knew it was against the law, but that it was sometimes done anyway. She didn't know how. She wondered what her parents would think about it—would they think it was a crime, or the best thing to do, considering her age?

She heard her father in the front hall and ran out to tell him where her mother was. As she expected, he was annoyed.

"Don't worry—I'm fixing dinner, Dad. It's just about ready now."

He looked pleased. "Well, I'm glad Betty didn't ask you to go along too."

"I guess she didn't want to call me out of school." She laughed a little nervously.

"Well, that's saying something for her," he said.

"Mom said she didn't think it was too serious."

"It wouldn't have to be for Betty to call your mother."

They ate at the kitchen table. Her father had taken off his tie and rolled up his sleeves; the September evening was warm.

"How is school?"

"Oh—it's okay. We get a lot of homework, but my teachers are okay. I'm not going out for chorus this year, though. I don't have the time any more."

"I can't believe you're a senior."

"Well, it always comes before you expect it, I guess."

He ate slowly, perhaps because of the heat.

"Is it all right?" she asked.

"Oh, yes. It's fine."

He continued eating. She felt uneasy about the silence. How strange to feel so uncomfortable with your own father!

"How was work?" she asked finally.

"Busy. They turned off the air conditioning too early so it was hot all afternoon."

"Oh, that's too bad."

She ate, hardly tasting the food. Her father had things to be annoyed about, she thought; her mother gone, and a hard day at work. But he wasn't taking it out on her. He never did. He just acted kind of distant, as though his business and his worries were things she could never begin to understand.

She got up to get some water. She stood at the sink watching him eat, his back to her. There was something steady about him. He seemed calm, as though he'd always know what to do. She didn't know why there wasn't more warmth between them, especially the last two or three years.

"Dad—" she began.

"This is very good," he said. She had also cooked a package of frozen peas. "I didn't know you could do anything in the kitchen."

"Well, I just heated up the meat loaf from last night, Dad."

"I thought I'd be in for a sandwich with your mother out."

"I'm not that bad, Dad. I can light an oven."

"Oh, I know. It's just funny seeing you in the kitchen. It reminds me of the time—you were about seven—I found you standing on a chair by the sink trying to make Jello with cold water."

"Well, I hope I've learned something since then," she said. "You know, a lot of girls my age can cook and keep house."

He laughed, not unkindly. He really seemed to find the idea amusing.

"I mean—I'm going to be seventeen my next birthday. Lots of girls are married at seventeen."

"Not many. Not these days, Phoebe."

"They *are*, Dad. Seventeen, eighteen, nineteen. . ."

He smiled. "I can't quite imagine you taking on a household. I don't think you know the problems involved. You're a little too young to handle problems like that."

She decided it was no use arguing the point.

"Besides," he went on, "your mother and I can't give you up so soon. It's bad enough your going off to college. What are we going to do without our baby in the house?"

Take mine, she thought crazily.

It surprised her to hear him talk about hating to lose her, because they spent so little time together nowadays. She'd have thought he would hardly notice the difference when she was away. Could it be that he had already lost the little girl he remembered, and didn't want to be reminded of it by seeing her as she was now? Why was it so surprising to him that she could warm up a dinner her mother had made the night before?

"Dad—" she began again. She wanted to get the conversation onto a more serious note, although she didn't dare bring up the real problem. "I—I wanted to talk to you. I—hardly ever do, I know. I—maybe Mom has talked to you about me coming in too late."

"Well, nothing much," he said. "She thinks you stay out a little too late."

It was all so inconsistent! If he still thinks I'm a kindergartener, why doesn't he pay more attention to me coming in at two and three in the morning?

"I think maybe I *have* come in too late, maybe a few times. I mean, I think maybe Mom is right. . ."

He didn't seem to want to discuss it.

"Phoebe, I don't want to be too strict with you and make you come in earlier than your friends do. When I was your age my father was strict with me—too strict. I think he forbid a lot of things that wouldn't have done me any harm that I really cared about at the time. I think young people should have some fun when they're young, because there are plenty of responsibilities to worry about later."

"What did your father do?"

"Well, I had to be in the house every night by nine. And I couldn't play outside after school until my homework was done. Then by the time it was finished it was too dark out to play."

She hardly ever thought of her father being her age, and she knew she should feel grateful to him. It was good of him to want his child to have more freedom than he had. He just didn't realize that she had almost *nothing* to go by.

"Of course my father thought he was doing the right thing," he went on. "They had different ideas about how to raise children in those days."

How funny that he should still think of her as a child, and at the same time allow her so much freedom.

Maybe he thinks a little girl can't possibly get into trouble, even if she stays out half the night with a boy, she thought.

She was sure her mother thought differently about that, although she never said anything.

"Would you make me some coffee?" her father said. "Just some instant."

The phone rang and she answered it. It was her mother, saying she was at her sister's. The child was fine, and she would be home in an hour.

She gave the message to her father. He said nothing, and went into the living room and turned on the television. She brought the coffee to him and thought about staying, but she could tell he was annoyed by the phone call and didn't want to talk any more.

She started to go up to her room, then remembered the dishes. She cleared off the table, and washed the plates and silverware in the sink. Then she went upstairs.

It had been the first time she had talked with her father in some time, and he had been nice—very nice, considering the bad mood she knew he was in. But it seemed more impossible than ever to talk to him about what was really on her mind. She could imagine the feelings of affection he had for his "little girl" turning into fury when he discovered the daughter he really had.

She started doing her Spanish assignment, but felt drowsy and fell asleep on her bed with the book open beside her.

She woke up—she didn't know how much later—to the sound of angry voices downstairs. Her mother was home and she could hear her father shouting something. She heard, ". . . more responsibility for your sister than you do for me. If you cared more about me, you wouldn't let her take advantage. . ."

And her mother saying, "He needed ten stitches on his foot! Betty was hysterical! What could I do? I'm not going to turn my back on my own flesh and blood just to please you."

Then her father said something about how hard he worked and how little she appreciated it. And her mother said something about housework, and then something about money that didn't seem to have much to do with anything. But money, Phoebe had found, often came up when her parents quarreled.

They didn't quarrel often, but when they did it was usually quite bitter. Neither one of them was the type to come right out with it the minute something bothered or jarred. They never had little spats to clear the air. By the time they *did* say something, there was a lot of stored-up resentment in every word. Betty's "emergencies" had annoyed her father for years, but he rarely said anything about it.

Sometimes Phoebe had listened to her parents arguing with a kind of horrified fascination, following them like a tennis match, trying to figure out who was right. Often she had sided with her father, thinking that if she were only in her mother's place, she would make him so much happier. She'd never let him come home to an empty house. She'd never complain about housework, or nag about money or anything the way her mother did.

Lying on her bed, she saw the rag doll that used to sit on her bookshelf. Her mother must have put it on her pillow when she made the bed. It suddenly made her think of a story her mother once told her out of Phoebe's own childhood.

When she was a little girl she had a favorite doll she called Annie. She played with Annie, talked to her, occasionally hit her, and wouldn't go to sleep without her.

After a year the doll was a wreck. She had a cracked face, bald patches, and an arm that hung by a few threads. But for all her parents' cajoling, nothing would persuade Phoebe to give up this particular pet. Until one day her father saw a doll in a store that looked just like Annie. He bought it, didn't show it to his daughter, simply pointed out instead all the things wrong with old Annie and this time said she would have to go to the hospital. Phoebe finally agreed. A day or two later her father gave her the new doll, saying it was Annie returned from the hospital. Phoebe was overjoyed. All the sins she had committed against her constant companion were repaired.

She didn't know now if she remembered all this, or just thought she did from what her mother had told her. But she did remember the strange kind of pleasure she took in the idea of her father giving her the doll. It was like his giving her a baby. The thought made her feel guilty when she thought of her mother, but she thought it all the same. It was the same kind of pleasure she felt during those arguments, when she took her father's side against her mother, thinking she would do better in her mother's place.

But listening to them argue now, she felt frightened. It sounded to her as though they hated each other, and if they hated each other, they must hate her too, because she was part of them both. At least that's how she felt. She didn't want to take her mother's place. She regretted even having had the thought. She wanted her parents to love each other, and be happy, and to see her as their child, no older than she was and no younger than she was. And somehow to help her.

The quarrel came at a bad time for her. It wasn't violent; it was a quarrel like those many married couples have from time to time. But every angry word made her wince. She hugged the pillow to her, then the rag doll, and clenched her teeth to keep from crying. She started crying anyway. She felt so helpless as she heard her parents' voices rise and fall.

9

"YOU BETTER hurry up, Phoebe. She just blew the whistle."

Jennie Unger seemed to slam the door of her gym locker, slip on the combination lock, and fly out to the gym all in one and the same minute. Phoebe stood by her open locker. She was in her blue gym suit and white socks, and held her sneakers in one hand. She was the only one left in the girls' dressing room. She was going to be late. Yes, there was the second whistle.

She decided to get an excuse from the class, even though she should have done it earlier. She would say she had cramps.

It's just as well to miss this one, she thought.

Miss Dalton had the ropes hanging down from the ceiling of the gym, and she was probably going to get the class to practice climbing. They had done a little of that in junior year. It seemed strange to Phoebe that she had enjoyed it then. Now she was afraid of getting dizzy or nauseous high off the ground on a swinging rope. And all you had to do was worry about an accident and it was sure to happen.

She hadn't seen her father at breakfast. He had left for the office before she came down to the table. Her mother

61

had said nothing about last night. She had just put a box of cereal on the table, hardly looking at Phoebe. Her eyes were red. Phoebe hadn't asked her anything about Betty, or her little boy, or anything connected with the day before.

She took off her gym suit, put it back in her locker, and put her skirt and blouse back on. Then she went down to Miss Dalton's office. Miss DeNero, the young assistant teacher, was at the desk.

"Miss DeNero, I have to be excused from class. I have cramps."

The young woman looked up from her book. Phoebe tried to look as though she were suffering a good deal of discomfort bravely.

"The whistle blew ten minutes ago. Where were you?"

"I put on my gym suit, Miss DeNero, then I had to get undressed again. I was going to take the class anyway, but my cramps were too bad. And, you know, it's rope climbing."

Miss DeNero said nothing, but wrote Phoebe's name and the date on a memo pad.

"Uh—and could I have a library pass, please?"

"All right. Next time you need an excuse, ask before the class starts."

"I will. Thank you, Miss DeNero."

She walked out into the hall, the library pass in her hand.

There were more people in the library than last time, and her old seat was occupied. She found a table that was empty except for one girl, and took the chair across from her. She hesitated only a minute before going to the encyclopedia again. There was something she had started thinking about. She had wanted to look it up all day. She got Volume A from the shelf and opened it to the article on abortion. She kept one finger on the next page, ready to turn to "Abraham, the first of the Hebrew patriarchs," just in case.

What she read about abortion confused her at first:

> Several studies indicate that approximately ten per cent of all pregnancies terminate in abortions. Early abortion may occur before the young pregnancy has formed a secure attachment to the uterus. Many early abortions are not recognized as such by the patient or her physician because they may occur without recognizable symptoms.

To her, abortion meant an operation. This made it sound like a natural process.

> The abortion process may start with pains in the lower abdomen, similar to menstrual cramps, and slight bleeding. . . In other cases, the abortion process begins with more severe cramps and profuse bleeding, which indicates a rapid separation of the gestational sac from the uterine lining, and its expulsion from the uterus.

The way they were using "abortion," it must mean miscarriage. Her Aunt Betty had had a miscarriage, she remembered. The last paragraph touched on what she wanted to know. She drew her breath as she read it:

> In many countries, including all fifty states of the United States, a person who willfully causes an abortion in the absence of accepted medical indications is liable to conviction of crime. The annual number of criminal abortions is unknown, but they contribute much to invalidism and death. When abortions are performed under unsanitary conditions, a common complication is infection, which may result in the inability to have children.

She closed the book and, because she didn't want to keep sitting at the table, took it back to the shelf. Maybe they just put that in to frighten people. If so, it worked.

63

She walked over to the window and stood looking out at the street in front of the school. It was drizzling, and a few people passed by with brightly colored umbrellas. A policeman in a shiny black mackintosh was directing traffic at the corner.

She had forgotten to bring an umbrella. Usually her mother would have reminded her, but not this morning.

I have to be careful not to get colds, she thought. What if they called the doctor? Maybe he can see signs other people don't notice.

"No standing by the windows," said a voice from the librarian's desk.

"I had to sharpen my pencil," she said. But since she had no pencil with her she returned to the table.

She had no classes with Paul but they usually met after school and got a ride home from a friend of his, Pete Roemer. She wanted a ride home but she didn't want to see Paul now.

In sixth period geometry class she asked her friend Joanne for a ride.

"Don't tell me you're talking to me again!" Joanne said with mock enthusiasm. "I thought you spoke to no one but Paul Mackley. Plus I thought your family must have moved to Alaska."

"What do you mean?"

"I'm always trying to call you. I tried to call you last night, the night before—no one answers."

Phoebe thought of herself locked in the steaming bathroom while the phone kept ringing.

"Oh, my parents and I must have been over at my aunt's."

"Are you feeling all right? I'm going to lend you my sun lamp if you look like that tomorrow."

She met Joanne at her locker after school and waited about ten minutes while her friend got organized. Another girl joined them. Joanne was giving her a ride home too. She and Phoebe stood around while Joanne made a series of rapid decisions about the contents of her locker. This included books, notebooks, a box of cookies, white shoe polish, three sneakers, a lunch bag, a gym suit, and a drum majorette's hat. "What the hell is this?" she muttered each time a new possession turned up, holding it up to consider the question, then usually throwing it back into the locker.

The other girl was a junior, a tall girl with straight blonde hair. Phoebe had seen her in the halls but didn't know her name.

"Oh, are you the one who's going with Paul Mackley?" the girl asked when Joanne finally introduced them. "He's adorable!"

After Joanne let the girl off at her house, Phoebe told her she wanted to come over to her house after supper, as she had something she wanted to discuss with her. Having said that much, she felt confused and didn't want to say anything more. She forced herself to look at Joanne, who was watching the road ahead and slowly chewing gum.

Phoebe looked at her friend in despair. She needed to talk to someone wise, someone kind, someone older. But she had thought of everyone she knew, and Joanne was the only one she could think of to confide in. Why should that be? Was it because the world was like that, or was it something about her?

10

SHE WENT straight up to her room and lay down on the bed, glad of a chance to close her eyes at last. The next thing she knew her mother was calling her down to dinner. She had been sleeping for three hours. At the table her parents were quiet. She could tell from their voices, when they did speak ("please pass the bread"), that they weren't angry any more, but each one seemed hurt and reproachful of the other. Phoebe sat between them and couldn't think of anything to say. Asking for news about her cousin seemed like a bad idea, and so did everything else that came to mind. Everyone ate quickly. There was the monotonous clicking of knives and forks on china that one never notices when people are talking.

"I'm going to Joanne's to do homework," she said, looking at neither one of them. "She said she'd give me a ride home after."

"All right," said her mother. Her father pushed back his chair and went into the living room.

Joanne's bed was covered with stuffed animals. She lay on her stomach, her head propped up in one hand, looking at Phoebe. She was chewing gum again.

"So how do you like being a senior?" she asked. "You haven't even been over once since school started, you know."

It was true. They used to see each other nearly every day. That had changed during their junior year, when Phoebe started going with Paul.

"It's great," said Phoebe.

"Too bad Andre caught you in history. You should have at least tried to guess. Where's your fighting spirit?"

"I wasn't even listening to her. I didn't feel good."

Joanne said nothing, she seemed to be waiting. Phoebe felt her mouth go dry, as though it were full of cotton. She knew she was about to take a step she couldn't take back. There was the mental picture of a cat being let out of a bag. Who was the cat? Who was the bag?

Who was Joanne? A good friend, right? Since kindergarten.

"Joanne, I want to tell you something but you have to promise not to tell anyone. It's very important."

Joanne's eyes stayed fixed on her. Her mouth halted slowly as she stopped chewing her gum.

"What is it?"

"I'm in terrible trouble."

"What?"

"You have to promise."

"I promise. You know I can keep a secret."

If there were any choice, she wouldn't have told. She would have made up a phony "secret" that didn't matter and then gone home. She didn't know anyone in the world well enough to trust with this. But she had no choice.

"I'm in real trouble. I don't know what to do. I think I'm pregnant."

Joanne said nothing. At the word "pregnant," her eyes widened and her mouth fell open soundlessly.

"You can't be," she said finally in a kind of loud whisper. There was so much horror in her voice there was little room for sympathy.

"I know I am. I mean, I've skipped a period, a whole month, and now I'm—I don't know—I'm about forty days late."

"Oh, my God."

"I don't know what to do."

"Oh, my God. I didn't know..."

"I haven't told Paul. I don't know what he'll say. You're the only person I've told."

"My God, what are you going to do?"

That's my question, thought Phoebe. It was awful to hear it coming from Joanne.

"I don't know."

"You have to tell Paul, Phoebe." She paused, and turned her head, looking at a stuffed lion that had fallen onto the floor as if in distress at what he'd been hearing.

"It *is* Paul, right?"

Phoebe felt her face flush with anger, and then, for the first time she could remember, she had the feeling that she wasn't on an equal footing with her friend. She couldn't snap back, "What kind of a remark is that?" She couldn't risk a falling-out. She couldn't even think of walking out and slamming the door behind her.

"Yes, of course it's Paul," she said quietly. "You know I don't go out with anyone else."

"I didn't know, Phoebe. I always wondered how far you were going with him..."

Phoebe bit her lip. Again it was better to say nothing.

Joanne went on. "I mean, ever since you started going with him you seemed different, like you were in another world—I didn't know what was going on..."

"Joanne, I don't know what I'm going to do."

"Look, maybe you aren't. Did you go to a doctor?"

"No, I'm afraid to. I don't want to go to Jansen. He might think it was his duty to tell my parents, and then I'd never be able to stop him."

"But they've got to know sooner or later."

"Maybe not."

"But you have to get a test. You might be sick. It might be something else. It might even be serious, and you have to find out. . ."

It was as though Joanne could see no hope if Phoebe *were* pregnant, and had to hold out the idea that she might not be.

"I get morning sickness," said Phoebe. "It started a few weeks ago. I'm afraid to go to school some days."

"Oh God, I can't believe this."

The more upset Joanne became, the more Phoebe felt strangely calm. She heard her own voice, as though someone else were doing the talking—someone calm who was without emotion.

"Joanne, do you think your sister might know what to do? I have to go away somewhere and have it, or else get an abortion some way. I have to decide soon. I can't just wait."

"I'll call her," mumbled Joanne. She still wasn't looking at her friend. Then suddenly she got up and went over to where Phoebe was standing by the dresser.

"Oh, Phoebe, you poor kid!"

She hugged her. There were tears on her face. Phoebe saw them without much emotion. She had wanted sympathy, but Joanne's crying didn't help. She needed someone to be kind, but not to cry or be upset. If anyone was going to be a prima donna it should be she. She needed someone who would take a practical look at her situation, not judge her; realize the damage was done, and advise her what to do to make the best of it. She had forgotten how much of a shock the news must be. She had had weeks to get used to it gradually. The strange feeling of calm was even stronger. Joanne didn't have to hold back her tears; she did. Besides, she had already cried enough.

No doubt Joanne was crying because she felt sorry for her. But also because the thought of such trouble must have stirred up feelings and imaginings about her own life.

"Phoebe, don't worry, don't worry. We'll think of something. I'll call Marion. She'll know something. I'm so glad you told me—you poor kid, I don't know how you stood it. I'll call Marion."

"I'm afraid of someone hearing if you call from here. I don't want anyone to find out. You know, if it leaked out some way it would be all over."

"Oh, sure. Don't worry about Marion."

Phoebe noted, as from a distance, that Joanne's concern about secrecy could never be as desperate as her own.

"Joanne, please don't tell Marion it's me. As soon as it begins to get away from me, you know, I feel like it's all out of my control."

"You can trust her, Phoebe."

"But I feel funny about her knowing. No one knew but me and now all of a sudden a lot of different people will know."

Joanne shrugged.

"Please just say it's a girl in your class. Someone she doesn't know."

"Okay. If you want."

"Do you think she might know something? Did she ever say anything to you?"

"No. But, you know, she knows a lot of girls at school, and you always hear about college girls. Anyway, she's going to know more than I do or you do, right?"

"I guess so. I hope so."

70

Joanne sighed, and sat down on the bed again, staring at the shaggy pink rug at her feet.

"I still can't believe this," she said.

Phoebe said nothing. She wanted to go home and be by herself. She dreaded the call but she knew she shouldn't put it off.

"Listen," said Joanne. "I'm going to go down and get us something to eat. Then we can talk it over up here and you can get calmed down." (Phoebe was as calm as she would ever be.) "Then we can go out to Holly's and call from a pay phone."

"All right. Thanks."

She heard her friend bound down the stairs. So now someone else knew. It was funny she didn't feel more relieved about having told her. It was still her problem as much as ever. But maybe the call would help. She took her hand away from her mouth and looked disgustedly at the nail of her little finger. It was bitten down to the quick. Some of the others weren't doing so well either. She'd been biting her nails without knowing it.

In a couple of minutes Joanne was back, pushing the door open with her foot and holding two bottles of soda and some potato chips in her hands.

"We'd better go to Holly's, all right," she said. "We can't call from here. My mother and father are in the living room watching the tube."

"Then let's go to Holly's."

Joanne put the bottles down on a table by the bed. She seemed to be looking at what she was doing, but Phoebe knew she was really looking at her.

"You know, Phoebe, you'd never guess by looking at you."

It was true. She had put on her blue jeans and a sweater before coming over. They were pretty tight but nothing showed.

"I know, but that won't last long."

"I guess you're right."

"Once it starts, it really gets out of control," she said. "I've seen some pictures of it."

Joanne had kicked off her loafers and gotten comfortable on the bed, using a giant panda for a pillow. She was drinking her soda thoughtfully. Now that the first shock had worn off, it looked as if she wanted to have a long girl-to-girl talk about it. Phoebe sat down on the edge of the bed, and ate some potato chips and drank some soda, feeling as though she were at some kind of insane pajama party.

"How come you never said anything to me before?" asked Joanne.

"I haven't been sure that long."

"No, I mean about you and Paul."

"Well, I felt like it was just between him and me," Phoebe answered.

"But now it's not."

"No, now it's not."

"What I can't understand, Phoebe, is didn't you think what might happen? You know the facts of life as well as me. I thought better. How could you just go ahead?"

"I thought of it. But, you know, I got away with it a few times, if you want to put it like that, and pretty soon it didn't seem like anything would happen."

"Did he force you into all this?"

"No. He wanted to but he didn't force me."

It wasn't a pleasant conversation. She ate a potato chip dutifully, as if the talk would be over as soon as the bowl was empty.

"When did you start? I mean, sleeping with him?" asked Joanne.

"Before school let out. Sometime in May."

"Where, in your house?"

Joanne was so genuinely interested she couldn't bother to think if her questions were embarrassing.

"No. You know, we spent a lot of time up at Greenwood Lake. We found a place up there that no one lives in any more."

"And what happened? Like all of a sudden you just got carried away?"

"No, we just got used to, you know, necking and everything, and it was kind of gradual. Each time go a little further—I never knew where to stop, I'd think if you've done this, why not that? One thing leads to another."

"Did you feel different after the first time?"

"Yes, I guess so."

"It's so funny I couldn't tell. It seems like it ought to show all over someone. You know, Phoebe—" her voice became quieter, confiding, "Mike tries to persuade me to go further all the time. He'd never stop if I didn't make him. But I just didn't think it was right. We got into some fights about it. I wish we had talked about them—you and me. I couldn't stand him pressuring me, but I know I did the right thing. We just neck in the drive-ins but that's it."

"I know I did the right thing." Joanne had said that with some satisfaction. And why not? She had had a choice to make too. Phoebe had done one thing and she had done the other. And sometimes Joanne had wondered whether she was right, whether she was missing something just because of fear, or old-fashioned ideas. Phoebe's news could only make her feel surer than ever that she *had* been right—no matter what Mike might say to her from time to time. It's only human nature to enjoy having been right, but it isn't especially pleasant for the one who made the other choice. Phoebe could hardly defend hers now.

It's so easy to feel superior, she thought. For some

73

reason the name Sue Driscoll flashed into her mind. She knew the name but she couldn't even connect it with anyone she knew.

"But, you know, Phoebe—I never really liked Mike that much. I mean, we still go out but we're not really in love. We don't ever talk about getting married, even as a joke. We kid around a lot. But I could tell you were more—I don't know, serious about Paul."

"That's why it happened. We were both serious. I'm not so stupid, you know."

Joanne nodded and sighed.

11

THEY DROVE out to Holly's and parked in the big parking lot outside the low steel and glass building. Holly's was sort of a super-diner, and very popular with kids who had just gotten their cars. There was no way to get to it on foot. Phoebe and Joanne were walking past the juke box toward the phone booths in the back when they saw two boys they knew—Bob Westenberg and Joe Dennis—sitting at a booth. Bob called over to them.

"Hey, Phoebe, I want to help you with your homework!"

She lifted her hand in a brief wave and forced a laugh.

"Everyone I see today is a history expert all of a sudden."

She wanted to go straight to the phone, but Joanne stopped.

"Let's go over and talk to them a minute," she whispered. She headed in the boys' direction and there was nothing to do but follow.

"You girls here alone?" asked Joe.

"Alone together," said Joanne cheerfully. The boys moved over and the girls slid into the booth beside them.

"Where's Paul?" Bob asked Phoebe.

"Homework," she said, hoping he hadn't been at Holly's with any of his friends. "Joanne and I were studying and we just came out for a soda."

"We were just having a discussion about whether Parker is classically insane or just neurotic," said Bob.

Joanne laughed. Mr. Parker taught the chemistry class Bob and she were in. Phoebe had never had him for a teacher.

"Listen," said Joanne. "Just because you might fail chemistry doesn't mean the teacher is insane."

"No, honestly," said Bob. "I'm being as objective as a scientist. I think there's something wrong with him mentally. He's always giving me these strange, like frightened, looks."

He demonstrated a strange, frightened look. Joanne laughed.

"Maybe that's because you've wrecked so many of your experiments. What is it now? Three? And school only started a month ago. Do you blame him for dreading the sight of you? After all, he's got sulphuric acid, potassium nitrate, and a lot of other things around, and sooner or later he knows he's got to pass some out to you. No wonder he can't sleep."

"A couple of beakers broke but none of it was my fault," said Bob.

He was known for being very clumsy. Everyone laughed.

"Listen," said Joanne. "I was miserable I didn't get you for a lab partner, but I began to realize it was good luck in disguise when I saw that first job you did. So what if I got someone who was far less strong and handsome than you. . ."

This wasn't the night Phoebe would have picked for Joanne to start something with Bob Westenberg.

". . . but at least I'm not in actual physical danger,"

76

Joanne babbled on breathlessly. "I'm not nervous, and you don't go around telling people I'm classically insane —and besides, what do you mean by classical?"

"I'll play you something," said Bob. "What's your favorite song?"

Joanne slid out from behind the booth and headed for the juke box. Bob followed right behind her. Phoebe heard her saying, "What do they have? What do they have?" as she bent over the listings.

She stayed in her seat watching them. She couldn't think of anything to say to Joe.

"Do you feel okay?" he finally asked.

She started, then laughed for no reason, as though he'd said something funny.

"Oh, sure. I'm just getting tired. What time is it anyway?"

He looked at his watch.

"Ten after ten."

The Rolling Stones came on, flooding the place with a London-Tennessee twang:

Oh, doctor, please help me, I'm damaged!
There's a pain where there once was a heart. . .

"Oh, I love that," she said. "A song for every occasion." It was funny how many songs were about misery but they were so nice to listen to anyway. Most of them seemed to be about being left alone and not being able to stop loving the person who left.

She was getting nervous just sitting there.

"You know, there should be songs for everything," she said. "Not just the usual things like 'I love you' or 'Why don't you love me?' but more specialized, naming names, like 'I hate Sam Daley but I like John Bertone so I'm going to start going out with John if he asks me, but not

Sam. My own name is Sylvia Bradley.' And stuff like that."

Joe laughed, giving her a puzzled look.

"I've got to be honest with you, Phoebe. I'm glad they don't have songs like that. The world is tough enough as it is."

"Well, how about—" She wanted to keep talking but the next thing she thought of was 'I'm worried to death because I think I'm pregnant, but maybe a miracle will happen and I'm really not after all; if I am, and I probably am, I'll probably have to get an abortion or else go to some kind of home and then give up the baby for adoption, or maybe my parents will kill me. My name is Phoebe Altman.'

"I can't think of another good one," she said. "But that's the idea."

"Do you and Joanne hit the bottle much?" he asked.

"You've never seen me drink or you wouldn't ask," she said. "If I have two beers I can hardly walk."

"You're too clean-cut, Phoebe. You know Paul is a terrific drinker. Mike and Steve and Pete Dranner were out at Gerde's on Steve's birthday and Paul had more than anyone—I swear, I think he drank four of those quart bottles of Ballantine's ale—and he drove Steve's car home."

"I know he's a terrific driver," she said. "Too bad he doesn't have a car. But you should see him hitchhike!"

"I've seen him do that too," said Joe. "He's a great guy."

Joanne and Bob came back. Joanne was excited. It was obvious she was extremely happy about running into Bob, but she seemed to remember herself when she saw Phoebe listening glumly to what a great guy Paul was. She stopped laughing and looked more serious. In a few minutes the boys wanted to leave, and she said they were going to stay a little longer. She and Phoebe watched them go out the door.

"I just think that Bob Westenberg is so adorable and I never get a chance to see him outside that lab class."

The call took less time than Phoebe had imagined it would. Holly's was almost empty, and she left the door to the booth halfway open so she could hear Joanne. First a long distance operator, then five quarters registering in the machine with a deep gong, different than for dimes, and then...

"Marion? It's Joanne—listen, Marion—I'm calling you about an emergency. I'm not at home. You can't tell Mom or Dad. Listen, a friend of mine, a girl in my class is pregnant. Her parents don't know and she doesn't want to tell them. She doesn't know what to do... No, she doesn't want to get married... No, of course it's not me—I swear it's not me. I'd tell you if it was... No, don't worry about me, Marion... You don't know her." She listened for a little while. Phoebe could hear sounds from the receiver but couldn't make out the words.

Joanne hung up.

"She said you should go to a doctor," she said, pushing back the folding door.

"Let's talk outside."

They went out to the car.

"She says you should get a test. Unless you get a test and it's positive, you don't even know if you *are*."

"What else did she say?"

"Well, it's silly to make plans until you know you *are*."

"What else did she say?"

"Well, she knows a girl who might know something, but she has to ask her."

They were driving along Bingham Street, on the way to Phoebe's house.

"Does she know anyone who had an abortion?"

79

Joanne was looking straight ahead at the road. Phoebe watched her.

"I don't know. I don't know if she'd tell me. She still thinks of me as a little squealer because of something I did when I was about five—but I think she can probably find out something. She didn't sound that surprised. It probably happens more at college than in high school... Look at that woman driver, she didn't even signal... I don't think it's happened too much at Midland, but, you know, maybe when girls drop out or move, that's what it is. The only girl I ever saw in school who was definitely pregnant was Sue Driscoll, and that was three years ago. We were freshmen, what a shock. I was in her gym class and I'll tell you, I couldn't believe my eyes. I don't know why she didn't quit before it got so obvious, 'cause she had to quit some time..."

Sue Driscoll. That was the name. She was a senior Phoebe's first year in high school. Phoebe remembered a very pretty, very popular girl. She was some kind of class officer, a cheerleader, in the Honor Society—and going steady with the captain of the football team, naturally. You always saw her around. She seemed nice, too. It was so funny to hear the rumors about her, to know they weren't true, to *know* nothing so awful could happen to such a lucky girl—and then to see her in the halls, holding her books in front of her, wearing full skirts and bulky sweaters, and still unable to hide what was happening to her body. She had finally left school in spring, a few months before she would have graduated.

"I had forgotten all about her," said Phoebe. "Whatever happened to her?"

"Well, she didn't get an abortion, that's for sure. She must have been five or six months when she was still in school. You know, an abortion has to be early or it isn't safe."

"I know. I heard that somewhere."

"But you know how Marion always went out for sports? Well, she said she was once after school and some of the girls on the volleyball team were talking to Miss Dalton about Sue—everyone knew she was pregnant—and one of the girls was saying how Sue was really a nice girl, and Miss Dalton said she knew she was and it was the nice girls who usually got caught."

That was unexpected humanity from Miss Dalton. Joanne took a left and they were on Phoebe's street. A minute later they were parked outside.

"Well, thanks for everything, Joanne."

"It's nothing, Phoebe. I just hope I can help."

"Thanks. I really need it. I won't forget it."

"I don't know how you can be so brave about it," said Joanne. "If I were you I'd be hysterical!"

They said goodnight and Phoebe went up to bed.

12

HER MOTHER's voice, calling from downstairs, woke her in the morning. It was eight o'clock. She had forgotten to set the alarm. She got up and dressed in a hurry, then ran down to breakfast. She told her mother she only wanted toast and a cup of tea (her stomach was upset and she thought tea would help). Her mother told her Paul had called last night when she was out.

She didn't get very far at school that day—just through homeroom period. Her stomach had felt worse and worse. On her way to English, her first class of the day, she became scared she might get sick in the classroom. There was a kind of sudden perspiration on her forehead and under her arms, almost as if she had a fever. It was like an enemy in her body; she couldn't control how she was going to feel from minute to minute. The one thing she knew for sure was she didn't want to be trapped in a room with a class going on. She turned around and headed for the nurse's office.

She asked for an excuse to go home.

"What's wrong with you?" Miss Wethers asked, not looking up from her desk.

"I've got a terrible stomach virus. I'm afraid I'll get sick in class I feel so nauseous."

Miss Wethers was always on the lookout for malingerers, but when she looked up and saw Phoebe's face she softened.

"I'd better call your mother to come and pick you up."

"Oh, don't do that, please." A lie came quickly to mind. "She's sick too. I think it's the same virus."

"You'd better lie down here then."

"I just live a couple of blocks away. Please, I don't want to worry my mother."

Thank goodness there wasn't going to be any trouble. The nurse filled out a form and told Phoebe to take it to the principal's office. Phoebe thanked her, delivered the paper to the office next door, and went to her locker for her jacket. She was out of the building in another minute.

It was a relief to feel the cool air outside. She walked a block, then stopped and looked back at the yellow brick building. At the near corner on the second floor were the windows of the room where her English class was going on.

Everyone in there but me.

Reading—what were they reading? *Romeo and Juliet*.

A couple of leaves were falling from the trees onto the grass in front.

Fall is really here. Summer's over. Was *Romeo and Juliet* based on a true story?

Her mother wasn't in the house. Probably she was out getting the groceries, or maybe over at her sister's. Phoebe went into the kitchen and got a box of soda crackers from the shelf. Saltines and cold ginger ale. Her mother used to give her that when she was small and had a stomach ache. Why shouldn't it work now? Sitting at the kitchen table, she drank a glass of ginger ale and ate about a dozen crackers, one after the other. She made a mental note not to drink tea any more. ("From now on I want ginger ale and crackers for breakfast, Mom. Put in a good supply and don't look at me like that.")

She went into the dining room, looked up Dr. Jansen's number in the phone book, and dialed it immediately without giving herself time to think about it and back down.

His secretary answered. Phoebe asked for an appointment.

"Who's calling, please?"

For a split second she thought of giving a false name, but of course it was ridiculous. The doctor knew her.

"Miss Altman. Phoebe Altman."

"The doctor has no time until Friday, Miss Altman. Is this an emergency?"

"No, not really."

"What is the problem?"

"Well, I—uh—need a check-up. I haven't been feeling too well."

"I see. I can give you an appointment for Friday. You're in school?"

"Yes."

Most of the time.

"How about three-thirty?"

"Yes. All right."

She hung up. Maybe that was the secret—just do things without thinking about them.

But now she had to keep the appointment.

She got another ginger ale from the refrigerator, and trudged upstairs thinking it over. Maybe it would be easy.

Dr. Jansen, I've been advised that I ought to have a test to find out if I'm pregnant. A frog test, I believe it's called.

The last time Jansen saw her was during the great

84

chicken pox epidemic that swept the eighth grade, but why should he be especially surprised?

"I see, Phoebe."

"And I must know right away. How fast can you get me the results? I want to avoid the bore of a long wait."

"I understand completely."

(With his distinguished graying hair he was a true man of the world.)

"Let's see. Today is Friday. I'll get the specimen over to the lab first thing tomorrow, and then I'll be able to give you the result Monday afternoon."

"That will be fine, Dr. Jansen."

"Is there anything about this you'd like to discuss with me, Phoebe?"

"No, there isn't, but I would like to remind you that I'm coming to you as your patient and this is confidential, and I expect you to respect my confidence—I believe that's mentioned somewhere in the Hippocratic oath, and—don't tell my parents."

"Your parents don't know of the possibility that you may be pregnant?"

"No, they don't because I don't wish to discuss it with them. After all, I'm an adult, and I don't share everything with my parents as I did when I was a child. That would be a little childish, don't you think?"

"Yes—Miss Altman."

"Now you'll want a urine specimen?"

"Yes, if it wouldn't be too much trouble. . ."

"Not at all, doctor. I'll speak to the nurse about it. And now I must be going. Until Monday. . ."

She concluded this conversation lying down on her bed, drinking the last of her ginger ale. Another version of the same interview began in her mind, in which Dr. Jansen picked up the phone as soon as the words "frog test" were out of her mouth, and she had to throw her self, crying and screaming, onto his desk, covering the dial of the phone with her body, begging him not to tell her parents. . .

This had to stop. These daydreams weren't doing her any good. They either gave her a false sense of security or made her feel like jumping out a window.

Besides, she had really told someone now. She had actually told Joanne everything last night. She couldn't decide whether it was better or worse than the scenes she'd been imagining.

A little of both.

The phone rang. It was someone from school, checking to see if she was really home. She explained that her mother was sick, and sleeping. She went into the living room and turned on the television. There was a rerun of "I Love Lucy," "The Loretta Young Show," and two game shows. Then the afternoon soap operas began. She watched "As the World Turns," "Search for Tomorrow," and "A Brighter Day," getting up only once to make a sandwich (her stomach was recovering), which she ate in front of the television. As "A Brighter Day" ended, her mother came in. It was three-thirty, and Phoebe realized she probably thought she'd just come back from school.

"What are you doing watching television?"

"Where were you?"

"Over at Betty's."

Phoebe looked away from the television for the first time in an hour.

"Well, I'm glad you sneaked home early," she said, meaning to be reproachful but starting to laugh for some reason. Maybe she was just relieved to have her mother back in the house.

Her mother giggled uncertainly and sank into the easy chair across from Phoebe.

"What are you laughing at? I guess you heard a little of what your father said about Betty the other night."

"That's the understatement of the year. If you wanted to make it any louder you'd have to get special equipment."

"I can't stand that sarcasm, Phoebe. What makes you so sarcastic? You didn't get it from me. If you knew the day I've had. . ."

"I'm not being sarcastic. It's true."

"Well, don't exaggerate. It was just a little argument."

"Oh, is that why you haven't been speaking to each other ever since?"

"We've been speaking."

"Sure. 'Pass the bread.' It's a lot of fun."

"Well, your father has always had his own ideas about Betty—about my whole family, as a matter of fact. . ."

"So I gather."

"Don't make a mountain out of a molehill. You know Daddy and I love each other, but we do have differences of opinion once in a while. . ."

Phoebe started laughing again.

"What are you laughing at? Are you mad or what? Will you get me a Coke? I can't move. I'm exhausted. I had to give those kids a bath—Betty was too tied up with the house—and it was impossible. My dress is still wet. Phoebe, what are you laughing at?"

Phoebe gave her the Coke. She could tell by something about her—the way she looked, something in her eyes, the way she was talking—that her mother felt better again.

"Now what are you laughing at? Your father and I aren't perfect, I admit, but. . ."

Phoebe was laughing for no particular reason, just relief that maybe her parents did love each other a little.

"*Your father and I aren't perfect. . .*" How human! Now

would be the perfect moment to say, "I'm not perfect either, Mom. In fact, I'm worried about something in particular right now. . ."

Her mother was comfortably relaxed in the easy chair, drinking her soda, and seemed in a mood to talk a while before it was time to start supper. But it was too nice the way it was; she didn't want to spoil it.

13

After dinner Paul called. He sounded as though something was on his mind.

"How are you?" he asked.

"Fine."

"I heard you left school. What's the matter?"

"I didn't feel too good. But I'm okay now."

"When am I going to see you?"

She didn't know if she wanted to see him or not. She had been putting him out of her mind as much as she could.

"Well, what about Friday?" she said.

"How about tonight?"

"I don't think so. I don't feel that great. I'm going to go to bed early."

"I heard you were at Holly's with Joe Dennis."

"Who told you that?"

"Never mind. Is it true?"

"No, I saw him there a couple of nights ago. I was with Joanne and he was there with Bob Westenberg."

"Oh."

"You know I don't go out behind your back."

"If you say so. You just don't seem too dying to see me. So, Friday?"

"Yes."

"Okay, I guess I'll see you in school, or I'll call you about the time."

He said goodbye and hung up before she did.

Joanne picked her up at eight o'clock and they drove to a candy store in the next town to make the call. Joanne too had heard that she had left school.

"It was that damn morning sickness," Phoebe explained.

"Oh, no. Did you get sick?"

"I would have if I'd stayed. I said it was a stomach virus. Wethers took one look at me and that was all she needed."

They went into the little store and walked toward the back where there were two old phone booths. The store was almost empty. The owner, an elderly man, stayed behind the counter up front talking to his one customer.

Joanne dropped in the quarters and dialed. Phoebe got halfway into the booth with her.

"Marion? It's Joanne . . . You did? . . . She doesn't know yet. Well, can't you tell me anyway? She doesn't know yet. She's afraid to go to a doctor . . . Well, do you know the name of a doctor? . . . Why not? . . . Tell me now and she'll get the test . . . Why not? Well, what did *she* do?"

Joanne's look had been directed at Phoebe throughout, her eyes rolling with frustration.

"Marion, how can I tell you why? She hasn't gone and she doesn't know how long. . ."

Phoebe's eyes darted nervously from Joanne to the phone to the man behind the counter. Joanne kept talking.

"How do I know? She doesn't know herself!"

Phoebe grabbed the phone.

"Hello, Marion? It's Phoebe. . ."

Marion had known her since she was seven.

"Joanne is calling for me. I'm sure I am, but I'm getting a test on Friday."

"Phoebe?"

"Yes."

"Well, Phoebe." Marion seemed surprised, but not as shocked as she'd feared. "I'll do what I can . . . How far along do you think you are? Your parents don't know?"

"No. Please don't say anything to anyone."

"Phoebe, I know of a girl who had an abortion last year, but I couldn't reach her today. I think she lives in Philadelphia now."

"Would you try to get her, Marion?"

"Oh, I'm so sorry about this. How are you? You sound like you're holding up pretty well."

"I'm okay. Please try to call her."

"I will. Listen, call me when you have the results of the test. It might not be a good thing to do, you know, I mean an abortion. You have to know how many weeks along you are. . ."

"I know."

"It costs a lot, you know. I heard something about six hundred dollars."

She didn't have fifty dollars, but for some reason the money didn't worry her. It seemed the least of her problems.

"Phoebe, I know of another girl here who left school to have a baby. She went to a kind of special home in Vermont and lived there until the baby came. Then it was adopted right after it was born. . ."

"I don't know anything about those places, Marion."

"Well, maybe that would be the best thing for you. I

could go ask the school psychologist about that. It's perfectly legal. An abortion is another story, you know."

"I know. But this girl went to someone, a doctor, and she was all right?"

"Yes—you know, some of these doctors are a lot better than others. I just don't know about this. . ."

"Please, please try to find out. I just can't bear for my parents to know."

If she went to Vermont for a few months, her parents would have to know. If she got an abortion, she could always think of some story to explain being away a day or two, maybe with Joanne.

"I'll do what I can, Phoebe. Call me soon, all right? I won't call your house."

"Thanks, Marion. Good night."

She hung up and stepped out of the phone booth, releasing Joanne who had been trapped in the corner. They left the store, Phoebe feeling a little uncomfortable about what the owner, now alone behind the counter, might have heard. Well, he didn't know her.

They got into the car. Joanne suggested going to a drive-in hamburger stand on the highway. She seemed to think food could improve any situation, and sometimes Phoebe agreed with her.

"I thought you didn't want her to know," said Joanne.

Phoebe sank back into the car and stared ahead at the neon sign of the candy store.

"I was afraid she wasn't going to do anything."

"What did she say?"

"I guess the same thing she told you. She knows a couple of girls who got pregnant while they were at school. One of them had an abortion and the other went to some kind of home for unwed mothers and had it there. She's going to try to find out the names—I mean the name of the doctor and the name of the place."

"Phoebe, maybe you should go to a place like that. You could put the baby up for adoption and you wouldn't have to worry what happened to it. Lots of married couples want them and can't have them. It would have a great home—probably better than ours."

Phoebe smiled ruefully, and said nothing.

"I'm not kidding. . ."

"I don't want to have it. I don't even think of it as a baby. I think of it like being sick—and I don't know why I have to tell my parents and make them hate me, and drop out of school. . ."

She heard her voice rising. Probably most people would think she should be shot for talking like that. But it was how she felt. She didn't want a baby. She might have had some daydreams about it once, long before she started having sex with Paul, but once the risk of pregnancy became a real danger to her, the daydreams stopped. She knew she didn't want a baby now. She wanted her life to go on as it had been before this awful thing started.

"It's your business, Phoebe. I don't want to scare you, but I once read in the papers that a girl died from it."

"I don't think it happens very often."

"Yes, but isn't it too much of a chance to take? I mean, the last year of high school is great, but after all, it isn't worth taking a chance with your life."

"No. It's—well, the real reason is I don't want my mother and father to know."

"But they'd probably understand! I mean, they'd have to."

"No, they wouldn't."

"What could they do? They'd have to help you."

"Look, I've thought about it. I can't."

"But your mother is pretty nice. And your father isn't so strict either. . ."

93

It was hard to argue because she couldn't even think about it calmly. The idea of her parents knowing was so appalling, she thought she would just go crazy if it happened.

"I'd kill myself if they knew."

"I don't understand that, Phoebe."

"Because it's not you."

Joanne turned into the drive-in. They ordered sodas and Joanne tacked on a hamburger.

"By the way," she said. "Guess who asked me out?"

"Bob Westenberg," said Phoebe.

"Right. He wants to go to a movie Friday, and he said why don't you and Paul come too."

"I don't know. I don't really feel like it."

"It would do you good. Just take a break and forget about this mess for one night. What are you going to do, si. home alone worrying?"

"I'm going to see Paul Friday. I'll ask him if he wants to."

"Are you going to school tomorrow?"

"I'm going to try."

A half hour later, while she was undressing for bed, she felt for the first time that she was uncomfortable without a bra. Her breasts were heavier and felt tender. She hooked her bra back on again and buttoned her pajama top over it. Lying in bed, trying to fall asleep, she reviewed the situation. She wasn't just waiting and doing nothing any more. But what had she accomplished? She wasn't sure, except that now Marion knew.

14

THURSDAY NIGHT she spent at home, alone in her room, pretending to be doing homework. She had gone to school that day and nothing had happened. A few kids asked what was wrong with her the day before, but no one seemed suspicious when she mentioned a virus. She was always expecting that her upset stomach would be a dead giveaway.

Tomorrow she'd have to go to Dr. Jansen's office right after school.

She took a shower and got into her pajamas right after supper. She could hear laughter from the television downstairs, and closed her bedroom door so she could think. She wanted to go over in her mind what she was going to tell the doctor. She wouldn't have time in school. And she had to think about it realistically. He was a doctor. He wasn't going to be emotional about it. He wasn't going to love her or hate her, whatever her daydreams.

What questions would a doctor probably ask?

Dr. Jansen: Why do you need this test?
Phoebe: To find out if I'm pregnant. I'm quite sure I am.

Dr. Jansen:	What makes you think you are?
Phoebe:	My period is very late.
Dr. Jansen:	How late?

This was the kind of thing she should be able to tell him exactly. She went to the bookshelf and took her marked calendar from the Nancy Drew book.

Today was September 30. She counted the days from August 9, the first day she was late. She counted again to be sure. Fifty-one days.

Phoebe:	Fifty-one days, Dr. Jansen.
Dr. Jansen:	Fifty-one days since your last menstrual period?
Phoebe:	Uh no—fifty-one days *late*. Eighty-one days since my last menstrual period.

Dr. Jansen would certainly see she knew what she was talking about.

| Dr. Jansen: | You had relations with someone and didn't use contraceptives? |

That wouldn't be so easy to answer. Well, in a way it would. The answer was yes. If he asked *why*, that wouldn't be so easy to answer.

The first time she slept with Paul, the fear of pregnancy was very real. It always was, along with all the other worries she had about it. After the first night they had actually slept together, she thought of going to a doctor in another town, getting a fake gold band, telling him she was married and getting birth control pills or a diaphragm. It was like one of those daydreams. Something stopped her from actually doing it. Partly embarrassment, partly fear of being found out. Partly a dread

96

of being so sneaky. Where would she hide things like that? In her room? It struck her as so shameful.

There was something she hated about the whole idea. It made it all seem so *planned*. Once, Paul bought contraceptives (that proved he gave some thought to her) but she hated that too. If sleeping with him just happened, a natural consequence of their being alone together, she could think of all the good things about it. But the other way, with them both planning it, planning how not to get caught, made it seem so cold-blooded, like it not being just that they loved each other and nothing else mattered. It seemed less forgivable if you planned it. She put off thinking about it.

A week after that night, her period came on time, and it reassured her. They had crossed the line, done the most "risky" thing one could do, and it had turned out okay. When a few more months passed as safely, it confirmed her thinking that things would take care of themselves.

There were other reasons she didn't have a common-sense attitude about the risks she was taking. The whole thing had nothing to do with common sense anyway; it was hard for her to believe she ever *could* get pregnant. She just couldn't imagine it happening to her.

She knew some of the facts and thought she knew them all. She knew if her period came on time all was well. She knew something about ovulation—that there were only a few days of the month when a woman could conceive, and she knew the dangerous days came in the middle of the menstrual cycle. She figured out when these days would fall for her.

She had learned most of this from magazine articles she had read in the last couple of years, and the idea of the "safe days" did much to counteract the diagram Miss Dalton had presented to the hygiene class, which might have been entitled "How Easy it is to Get Pregnant." But the ideas she had picked up about the fertile days and the infertile days did her more harm than good. She had the false sense that nothing could happen as long as she and Paul didn't sleep together for those three or four days a month. She didn't know that her body didn't operate like clockwork, that many things could delay or speed up the process of ovulation, and that it was especially likely to happen at her age.

What day had she become pregnant? She didn't know, and the calendar couldn't tell her for sure. Her "dangerous days" after her last period had been July 24 to July 26. She didn't even see Paul those days; he was away in Maine on vacation with his family. In fact, he was away almost two weeks. He got back on a Saturday night. (It was already July 31, a perfectly safe day, according to everything she knew.) They had gone to the lake on Sunday and ended up on a cot in one of the upstairs rooms of the old house. It must have been then, even though it was supposed to be impossible. If it was then, she was two months pregnant now. If she had somehow become pregnant before Paul went away, she was more. She didn't know the dates of the other times. She thought it was twice, but that was a guess.

So she didn't know if she was two months pregnant, or two and a half months pregnant.

Dr. Jansen: How long ago did you become pregnant?
Phoebe: Two months, or two and a half months ago.
Dr. Jansen: Who is the father?
Phoebe: I'd rather not say.

All she wanted from him was a test, and maybe he would give her some advice. Better to go to him than to someone she didn't know. How would she know someone was a good doctor if she just looked him up in the yellow pages? A stranger might not be reliable—or something else might go wrong.

She put the calendar behind a picture in her wallet, so she'd have it with her in case she got confused. She tried to concentrate on that and forget about how much she dreaded the appointment.

15

IN SCHOOL on Friday, Phoebe hardly noticed that there was a history test (a surprise test, at least to her), and that she handed in a paper with ten out of twenty questions answered, all guesses. When the last bell finally rang, she left her homeroom immediately, made straight for her locker, and left. She was already three blocks away from the school and halfway to the doctor's office by the time most of the students were just leaving their homerooms.

She had been afraid she might not make it to the office on time, but when she sat down in the waiting room and looked at the clock, she saw she was ten minutes early. She picked up a copy of *Life* and put it down again when she saw the cover photo, an embryo labeled "The Miracle of Life." She picked up another magazine, this one with a cover picture of a crew of astronauts, and flipped through it. The pages sounded noisy in the quiet room.

A nurse came in and asked her to go into the doctor's office. Phoebe smiled, trying to look as if nothing special were on her mind, and walked toward the room. One leg felt like rubber.

Dr. Jansen was sitting at his desk. He stood up when

she came in and held out his hand. He looked a little older than she remembered him. She shook his hand and sat down.

"How have you been?" he asked.

"Fine. How are you, Dr. Jansen?"

"Older every day. How are your folks?"

It came to her that this honest, unsuspicious man might have the spirit of her father sitting on one shoulder, and the spirit of her mother on the other.

"You haven't been feeling well?" he asked.

"No, not too well."

"What bothers you?"

"Well, I've been feeling tired. . ."

He laughed a little. "I hear that very often from people your age. How much sleep do you get?"

"Uh—I don't know exactly. It's a little different every day."

Well, it's been nice talking to you.

"Is that all?"

"No—well—" She thought about her carefully worked out calendar. Now was the time to take it out and show him exactly what the situation was.

"I have a kind of psychological problem," she blurted out instead.

He waited for her to continue, but she didn't.

"What is it?" he asked kindly.

"Well—since you last saw me—you know, when I had the chicken pox, I got a boy friend—in fact, I started going with him last year. I'm a senior now, so is he—" she stopped again.

"What's the problem?"

"Well—" She had no intention of telling him the truth, but she found herself wanting to get close to it, like a moth circling around a flame. Maybe he would be able

101

to help her, slip her some kind of advice, without her actually admitting anything.

"There has actually been a big problem between us—about sex."

He didn't seem shocked.

"That's another problem people your age have, you know," he said.

He seemed to be waiting for her, but she said nothing.

"You have feelings that trouble you?" he asked.

"Yes."

"What kind of feelings?"

"I don't know. It's hard for me to talk about it."

"Have you had relations with the boy?"

"No," she lied. She hadn't paused for an instant.

"Do you feel guilty about wanting to?" he asked quietly. He was so understanding she hated herself for being such a liar.

"Yes, I do feel guilty," she said.

"Feelings like that are perfectly normal, Phoebe. It would be something to worry about if you weren't interested in sex."

"Yes, I know that, I guess."

"Are you worried about what to do?"

"Yes," she said, wishing she had come to see him a few months ago.

"Well," he said. "I can't tell you how to lead your life but I can talk to you about some of the situations I've come in contact with as a doctor."

He leaned back in his chair and started filling his pipe. He looked like the wise old doctor in the movies.

"Sometimes a girl no older than you comes here because she's gotten pregnant. Sometimes her parents bring her."

She kept her eyes on her hands, folded in her lap, and she could feel him looking at her. She wondered why he was going into this with her.

102

"Often people in this situation ask me about a way to terminate the pregnancy. It's not up to me to discuss the religious or ethical aspects of abortion, but I do tell them that the operation is illegal, except under very special circumstances in this state, and that it would be an illegal act for me to perform the operation or to refer them to anyone for that purpose. You see, when a girl is already pregnant, what I can do to help is very limited."

"Yes, I see," she said.

"All I can do is advise them about care during pregnancy. In some cases the girl gets married. In others she doesn't and in cases like that I advise giving the baby up for adoption."

"Yes, I see," she said again.

"I once had a woman come here with her daughter. For some reason she thought the girl was having relations with her boy friend, or was on the verge of it. The woman wanted me to tell the girl that sex before marriage was wrong and dirty and sinful and everything else under the sun. I couldn't do that. What I did say to her—and what I'm saying to you now—is that girls who go ahead and have a sexual relationship run the risk of becoming pregnant, and I've yet to see an unmarried pregnant woman who wasn't terribly sorry about it."

"Yes—I can imagine, Dr. Jansen."

"A girl in that situation doesn't have so many more faults than the rest of us. She isn't bad and usually she isn't particularly wild either. But she's made a serious mistake. She hasn't thought about the consequences of what she has done, and part of growing up is learning to be responsible for the things we do—to others and to ourselves. It isn't being responsible to a child to bring him into the world without a father. And a girl isn't being responsible to herself before she has a chance to decide what she wants to do with her life."

Was he trying to make her cry? She stared at the black marble paperweight on his desk, and tried to think of how to leave. She was glad to see him glance at his watch before he went on.

"A person has to be ready to take on a good number of obligations when he becomes a parent, Phoebe. Children need quite a lot from their parents, you know."

"Yes. Well, thank you, Dr. Jansen," she said, with a bright, unnatural smile on her face. She jumped up from the chair.

He stood up, smiling. "By the way, your face has improved considerably since the last time I saw you." He meant the chicken pox. "I can see you took my advice and didn't scratch."

"I tried not to."

She looked at him, trying to figure out if he had really guessed why she had come, and had been telling her indirectly that he couldn't help her get an abortion. But she felt sure from the way he talked and looked at her— so straightforward—that he hadn't. She had become quite good at concealing things.

"I'm glad you came to see me," he said. "It's better to worry now than later."

I worried both times, she thought. Before it was too late and after it was too late.

"I know this talk won't make the problem disappear, but I hope it has helped."

"It has. Thank you, Dr. Jansen," she said lamely, and walked to the door.

"Good to see you," he said.

She picked up her sweater, crumpled in a chair in the reception room, and left.

Please have the results by Monday, Dr. Jansen. It's such a bore to wait. And now I must be going.

The interview hadn't gone as planned.

A feeling of despair, quiet and desperate, fell over her as she started walking home. The air was still, as before a storm. It was getting dark early. The houses she passed, all with lights in their windows, looked warm and friendly. She imagined the people inside them had no worries.

Remembering the talk in the doctor's office made her feel ashamed. She felt a flash of blind anger at Dr. Jansen, then realized she wasn't angry with him at all, but with Paul. He didn't have to spend every waking minute lying and sneaking around and covering up and smiling when he didn't want to smile. He could afford to be honest and friendly and look people straight in the eye—a great guy, as anyone would tell you.

Three blocks from her house she passed the playground of the elementary school she had gone to. It was almost deserted. Swings, some seesaws, and a jungle gym stood unused, all in shadow. Two children played tag in back of the school building, further on.

Phoebe sat down in one of the swings, not wanting to go home yet. Paul had told her not to worry—she could remember his voice, his words, right now—everything would be all right, it was just between them, there was no reason to worry.

She imagined writing him a letter:

> *"You said you loved me, but you've hurt me more than anyone ever has. People like you just take what they want and never think about who gets hurt . . . I'm almost ready to kill myself. I wish I had the nerve. . ."*

Rocking slightly in the swing, she closed her eyes and put her head in her hands, waiting for the feeling to pass. She didn't want to hate him. It made everything seem even more meaningless.

And he didn't even know.

The swing was swaying unsteadily beneath her. She looked up and saw two children standing by the jungle gym, staring at her silently.

"What are you looking at?" she asked. "What's the matter?"

She got up from the swing, and picked up her books and the sweater she had laid on the grass. She continued on her way home, not looking back at the children. She didn't care what they thought.

She was supposed to see Paul that night. For a moment she thought of calling it off; then she decided against it. With some surprise she realized she was glad she would be seeing him. She didn't want to be alone tonight.

16

THREE HOURS later she found herself sitting in the back seat of Bob Westenberg's car with Paul's arm around her. They had gone to Courtney's drive-in because the boys had wanted to see *2001*. It had started to rain, and they were listening to the soundtrack over the steady squeak of the windshield wipers. Joanne and Bob were doing most of the talking. Occasionally Paul said something.

"It's a good thing I brought my umbrella!" Joanne said. "I'm going to get some popcorn." She turned and leaned over the front seat, asking Phoebe and Paul if they wanted anything.

"I'll get it," said Bob. "Don't you know how to act on a date? You're supposed to ask your escort."

Joanne laughed.

Bob simulated the correct way, using a mincingly lady-like tone: "Could I please have some refreshments?"

This threw Joanne into another fit of laughter. She was very excited.

"I'll never get what I want that way! Besides, I was trying to save you from pneumonia. After all, who's wearing the boots around here?"

She opened the door on her side and opened up her umbrella.

"I'll be right back with the goodies, kids," she yelled, and slammed the door. Bob hesitated a minute, then got out of the car with a sigh and followed her.

Phoebe felt Paul's arm tighten to give her a little hug.

"Nice to see you again." He bent his head down and kissed her cheek.

"It's good to see you too," she said, trying not to sound as sad as she felt. It really was good to be with him again. She had been avoiding him for almost two weeks.

"So what are you up to? Running around with Joanne again like when you were ten? Watch out—she's got a boy friend now too."

"I did homework over at her house a few times—that was all."

"Well, what's the point of that? I thought we had that all settled. You do your homework with *me*. I do mine with *you*. That way you won't get in trouble when you get called on in class. You're already showing the effects of this dumb decision. Do you think Joanne has a brain to equal mine?"

She could tell he was half kidding, half pleading with her. He knew something had changed in her feelings for him, but he couldn't figure out what.

"I saw Bob in school and he said you and Joanne wanted to go here tonight," he went on. "I would have rather seen you alone, but. . ."

She could tell he was worried by the anxious way he looked at her face as he spoke. When she didn't see him for a while, she could think of him as a reckless person who had gotten her into trouble because of his selfishness. When she was with him, she knew it wasn't that simple. She knew that he at least liked her, maybe loved her.

"Paul, I've been so miserable."

"I knew something was wrong. What is it?"

She said nothing.

"Something at home?"

"Yes," she said, wanting comfort and no more questions.

He put his arms around her and she rested her head on his shoulder for a moment. She had a funny split feeling; he felt so strong and comforting, but she didn't know if she could depend on it tomorrow or only for this minute.

"What, are your parents fighting a lot?"

She nodded and moved closer to him. Just a little warmth before going out into the cold again.

There was a knock on the window on Paul's side. The car door opened and Joanne piled in, holding four boxes of popcorn.

"I'm completely soaked—but I kept the popcorn dry. Here's yours. Bob got some root beer and some candy bars—now you've got to fill us in on the flick. Why is that guy floating around in space without a spaceship?"

"Ask Bob," said Paul. "He has already seen it a couple of times. I can't see a damn thing through the windshield, much less when you're there."

Bob came in the other door and passed out cans of soda and some candy. He glanced ahead at the screen.

"Oh, this is a very good part coming up." he said. "The computer on the spacecraft turns against the men on board, so it's a battle, with one of them trying to disconnect the wiring."

"I don't get it," said Joanne. "Do you think this kind of thing will ever happen?"

"Are you kidding? It's already happening."

"Did you get butter on your popcorn?" asked Joanne.

"I asked for some but I didn't get any—did you, Phoebe?" She swung around again in the seat, and gasped as she remembered something. "Guess who I saw at the refreshment stand? Anne Dobbs! And she's wearing a big black wig that belongs to her sister. I swear, I'd give her fifty dollars if she'd wear it to school. You'd die if you saw her..."

"Who was she with?" asked Phoebe.

"I didn't know him. He looked about twenty. Gee, why did that guy have to pick on me with this dry popcorn?"

"You want some of mine?"

"Oh, no, I shouldn't—hey, do you like this picture?"

"I do," said Paul. "If you could just sit down I'd like it a lot more."

"Brother, after everything I did for you, Mackley." She turned around and faced front.

Paul leaned forward and pulled her hair, forcing her to sit back.

"Sit down, Joanne. You never listen. I'm very sorry my girl friend is hanging around with you again because she's very impressionable."

"Ow! And I always warned her about you—or I should have."

"Now this part is very good," said Bob. "He's going into the computer's brain and pulling out the memory bank..."

"But why?" asked Joanne.

"Because they're on a collision course..."

"Oh, that wig! Phoebe, it was unbelievable—wasn't it, Bob?"

"Come on, watch the movie. This is a terrific part."

Phoebe sighed and ate her popcorn, giving the last of it to Paul, who had already finished his. Everyone quieted down and watched the movie. Phoebe rested her head against Paul's shoulder and closed her eyes. The sound of the rain on the roof and the squeak of the windshield wipers sounded nice, and with his arm around her she had a nice dreamy feeling of being protected and warm, just for a little while.

17

ON SATURDAY she woke up early and walked to the corner drugstore to call Marion. Again there was the voice of the long distance operator, the clang of quarters in the machine. Finally a sleepy voice answered. She heard some shouts in the dormitory hall; then the voice returned and said Marion wasn't there. She tried twice more during the afternoon. Each time someone else answered and told her Marion wasn't there. She was worried—it was a helpless feeling not knowing what else to do but keep calling the same number—but there was no reason to get upset, she told herself. It was Saturday. Marion could be at a football game, or any number of places.

Late in the afternoon, after the third call, she had a fight with her mother. It was the first in a couple of weeks. Mrs. Altman had somehow got the idea that her daughter's frequent trips out of the house meant she was smoking on the sly. Phoebe denied it, but her mother heard the guilt and evasiveness in her voice.

"I can tell when you're lying," she said angrily, looking up from the stove. "And I don't like it and you don't fool me. I won't stand for this sneaking around!"

"Why should I bother lying to you?" Phoebe yelled, desperately trying to take the offensive. "If I wanted to smoke I'd do it in front of you because I don't give a damn what you think! Do you think I'm afraid of you?"

She ran upstairs, feeling very afraid, and slammed the door to her room.

Paul called her before dinner but she told him she was sick and couldn't go out. She thought he believed her.

She spent Saturday night alone in her room. Her parents went out. At ten o'clock she tried to get Marion again, forgetting that the long distance call would show up on the phone bill. Another voice told her Marion wasn't there.

She finally got her on Sunday. She had forced herself to wait until noon before trying again. She closed the folding door of the phone booth and dialed the operator. While she waited for the call to go through, she saw people she knew, neighbors, coming in for the Sunday papers. She turned her back to the glass door.

A voice answered and in another minute Marion was on the line.

"Phoebe? Oh, I'm glad you called. How are you?" She sounded sleepy.

"The same. I've been trying to get you."

"I'm sorry, I was at a game yesterday. Did you go to a doctor?"

"Yes—and I definitely am."

"Oh, lord. Listen, Phoebe, I've got to tell you—I've been thinking about this and I'm sorry but I just can't help you with this abortion business. You know, it's risky, and if anything ever happened to you, your parents would never forgive me. It would be on my conscience..."

"Did you find out the name of one, Marion? Please, pleaso tell me. I'll be all right. Nothing will happen, and

113

I promise I'll never ever say anything to connect it with you. . ."

She was forgetting that she hadn't even started to figure out how she would get the money.

"I'm really sorry, Phoebe. But I did find out the name of that place in Vermont. Do you have a pencil and paper?"

"I don't want it, Marion. It's no use to me. My parents would have to know, I'd have to drop out of school. . ."

"I can't do it, Phoebe. I'm sorry. You'd better have a talk with your mother. Tell both your parents. They'll understand. You'll feel better when you've talked it over. . ."

"I'm not going to! I want the name of that doctor! Just give me the name and address."

"I don't have it, Phoebe."

"Please! I've had the test, Marion, and I'm definitely pregnant."

"I'm sorry, Phoebe. Call me if you want the address of that place."

There was a click at the other end of the line. She looked at the crumpled paper with the phone number of the college, and started to dial again. But when the operator came on, she hung up, realizing it was no use.

It was only then that she realized how much she had been counting on Marion's help. She had forced herself not to think too much about the operation. She had blocked out most of the fear connected with it. It had just been an idea to her—a means of rescue. And the idea had quieted her panic at the thought of her parents finding out. After Marion hung up, she realized she had no other plans at all. She felt a little dizzy. When she got home, she could hardly remember getting out of the phone booth and walking back.

Her parents had gone to a barbecue down the street.

114

There was a note from her mother saying Paul and Joanne had called. Phoebe drank a glass of water from the tap and tried to think. The phone rang and she reached out to answer it out of habit, then let it ring. There wasn't anyone she wanted to talk to.

Then she thought of someone. The name came to mind for the second time and this time she knew who it was— Sue Driscoll, the girl who became pregnant and had to leave high school when Phoebe was a freshman. It seemed somehow like a hope.

She looked in the phone book and found a listing for S. Driscoll at 226 Chester Street. It was at the other end of town, past the high school. She went up to her parents' bedroom and found her father's car keys on the dresser. She grabbed them and went out to the garage.

As she drove away from the house she began thinking about what she would say, how she would introduce herself. Should she give her real name? Should she explain how she knew about Sue, even though she was a stranger?

A car horn honked repeatedly. She started. A man passing on her left yelled something in her direction. She hadn't seen him trying to pass and had almost sidescraped him. Rattled, she pulled over to the curb and parked. She hadn't even seen the car. She would have to watch it. She sat still, trying to clear her head.

It was a quiet street, lined with trees that were turning orange and yellow. As she looked out the car window, she remembered something. It seemed so strange that she could hardly believe it at first. She didn't want to believe it, but she knew it was true.

When the rumor had first started circulating about Sue Driscoll, Phoebe had laughed about it. And she wasn't the only one. The giggling went hand in hand with whispers, at least among some of the freshman girls who didn't know Sue. To them she wasn't a person facing a terrible problem alone. She was a cheerleader, the president of this, and so-and-so's girl friend, who had tried to get away with something and been caught. The rumor was strangely exciting, a little frightening too, but you could think about it fearlessly because it was someone else, not you. All of a sudden everyone was hinting something about the girl's personal life that she had been keeping secret. As the weeks went on, they had only to look at her to know they were right. When they knew it was true, it seemed less funny. But none of them really knew how unfunny it was.

How strange to think that people might laugh at her now.

She started the car again and drove in the direction of the high school. Three blocks past it she came to Chester Street. It was an old neighborhood. She drove slowly, looking at the house numbers. 226 was two blocks down. She parked across the street from the house and got out of the car.

The house was old, with a screened porch in front. She walked up the wooden steps and rang the doorbell. She felt strange, like a different person, having the nerve to do this.

A woman in her fifties answered the door.

"Hello, I'd like to speak to Susan Driscoll."

"I'm Susan Driscoll," the woman replied.

"No—I mean, a Sue Driscoll who went to the high school a couple of years ago."

"You mean my niece. Are you a friend of hers?"

"Yes."

"Well, come in."

Phoebe followed her into the living room. She had heard that Sue lived with an aunt because her parents were dead or divorced or something.

"Won't you sit down?" the woman said, without looking at her. She left the room and Phoebe heard her calling up the stairs.

"Susan, a friend of yours is here."

She hadn't asked her name. Phoebe started to say, "My name is Mary Norton," but the woman didn't come back into the living room.

She heard footsteps on the stairs. She looked up and saw someone she had last seen walking in the halls at school. The girl stopped and looked at her with surprise. Phoebe didn't know what she had expected, but Sue didn't look very different from the way she remembered her. She still looked very young; her light brownish hair was worn the same way, maybe shorter. She was wearing a plaid skirt and a blouse that made her look as though she might still be in high school.

"I'm sorry. I didn't mean to barge in—you didn't know me but I knew you—I went to the high school, in fact I still do. . ."

"What do you want?" the girl asked. She seemed a little apprehensive.

"I—well, I'm sorry—I know I have a lot of nerve, but I'm so confused, kind of desperate—I know you had a baby, and I—I'm in the same situation. . ."

The girl looked at her with no change of expression. Phoebe couldn't tell what she was thinking.

"I know this sounds stupid but I was just thinking maybe you could give me some advice."

To her own surprise she started crying.

"What kind of advice could I give you?" the girl asked.

She looked directly at Phoebe as she spoke; it was impossible to tell if she was angry or hurt or simply didn't care. Phoebe remembered that she must have had a lot of pride, having had the nerve, or whatever it was, to keep going to school when she must have known people were looking at her and talking behind her back.

"I don't know. I wondered what you did—I heard you didn't get married."

"I didn't want to get married," the girl said.

It was hard to tell if it was true or not. Phoebe had heard that her boy friend didn't volunteer.

"I had the baby and my aunt and some other people persuaded me the best thing was to give it up for adoption, so I did."

"Oh, I see."

Phoebe had wanted to ask her the same question she had asked Marion, but she realized what a stupid idea it was. Why would Sue Driscoll know anything about a doctor who could clear it all up overnight? She had had the baby. Had she had a choice? Phoebe guessed not.

"That's all I can tell you," said the girl. "People will probably give you the same advice. It's supposed to be much better for the baby."

She wanted Phoebe to leave. Although she had told her what little she could, it was clear that she didn't welcome the intrusion, didn't welcome the reminder that complete strangers knew what had happened to her.

Phoebe recalled seeing her seated on the stage at some awards assembly. It must have been before she was pregnant, or at least before it started to show. The freshmen were just finding out who the big names in the school were, and Sue was one of them. She had worn a green sweater and a white collar; Phoebe remembered exactly what she had looked like. And you always saw her at football games and the pep rallies in the fall in the red and gold cheerleader's outfit. The girl walking to the door looked young enough for all that to have happened last week, but it must seem long ago to her now.

"I'm sorry to bother you," said Phoebe.

"No, I understand. It's all right."

The door shut and she walked back to the car. On the way home, she thought of going to see Joanne, but there was no point in it. She was too upset and it might upset her more. Her parents were still out when she got back.

She went upstairs and ran a hot bath, just for something to do. Her mind was racing, trying to think of something, anything, to stop the feeling that things were closing in on her. But this time it could come up with nothing. No names, no one to talk to.

She sat in the bath for a couple of hours. Her stomach was flat but it seemed just a little bloated, like it might be before her period. She couldn't decide if it was her imagination or not. She did know that some day, very soon, she would see a swelling, and that it wouldn't stop. She put on her pajamas and, having nothing else to do, lay down on her bed and cried.

Her parents came home late and went straight to bed. She hadn't been sleeping, but she kept the lights out and lay beneath the covers. She heard the door open. It must have been her mother looking in on her. She pretended to be asleep.

It was about eleven. The house was quiet. She tiptoed downstairs and went to the phone and called Paul. His father answered and seemed annoyed at her calling so late. Then she heard Paul's voice.

"Where were you? I was calling you all weekend."

"I've got to tell you something. I've been afraid to," she said, without stopping to think. "I'm pregnant."

She hung up, terrified to hear what he would say. She ran upstairs to her room and got back into bed, hugging her pillow. She was shaking. The phone rang downstairs. She lay still, praying it would stop. It kept ringing. In a moment she heard her parents' door open, and the light went on in the hall. She heard her father's heavy footsteps going down the stairs. In a moment he called her to the phone. She yelled down that she didn't want to talk to anyone. She was wild with fear. She didn't know what her voice sounded like.

After another minute her father called back that it was Paul and it was an emergency. She screamed that she didn't want to talk to him.

She heard her mother out in the hall, asking her father what had happened. She lay still, looking wildly around the dark room—at the closet, the window—there was no place to hide.

She heard her father coming upstairs, and some excited words between her parents. Her father rapped on the door.

"Phoebe! What's going on?"

She was too frightened to cry or even say a word.

"Open the door, Phoebe!" It was her mother.

She could hardly move from the bed, but she forced herself to get up. There was no lock and they would be coming in anyway. She touched the doorknob with a hand she couldn't steady, and opened the door.